Here's to Forever

TEAGAN HUNTER

Cover photo by Lindee Robinson Photography
Cover by Najla Qamber Designs
Models: Kelly Kirstein and Travis Robert Bendall
Editing by Indie Solutions by Murphy Rae
Formatting by AB Formatting

To Will Cooper.

You'll always be my number one.

#SorryNotSorryLake #BethWho

Chapter One

HUDSON

"You want to do what to my daughter?"

The man speaking to me right now like I've lost my mind is none other than Ted Kamden, AKA, my girlfriend's father. He's looking at me like I'm absolutely insane. He may be right.

Looking Ted right in the eye, I say, "Marry her, sir. I'd like to marry Rae."

Ted stares me down. Squinting his eyes and cocking his head, he says, "Why, son?"

Not what I was expecting.

I clear my throat. "Why, sir?"

"Yes. *Why* do you want to marry her? That's quite a commitment and you're both still young. Never mind the fact that you haven't even been together a year yet."

His words are true. We *haven't* been together that long, but for some reason it feels like an eternity that we've known one another.

A little less than a year ago, the brightest, snarkiest, and most beautiful woman I've ever known walked confidently into my shop.

She won my heart over almost instantly with her smart mouth and captivating forest green eyes. Our connection was easy, seamless, uncomplicated. It took a while for me to work up the courage to tell her about Joey, my now eight-year-old daughter, but once she got over the initial shock, Rae accepted us both with open arms. We became inseparable, in love, and infinitely happy.

Then life happened.

It turned out our intense connection came from the fact that we had already sort of known one another in the past, me having rescued her from drowning at the tender age of six. It wasn't until I took her to the beach for her birthday last year that we realized it. Being near the sea caused Rae to have a disturbing flashback where she discovered that her deep-seated fear of being a mother came from having her own stand and watch as she drowned.

The bigger, more present issue was Joey. As Rae came to her realization, my daughter waded into the ocean a little too far and got swept away in the angry waves. Joey nearly drowned.

It was two weeks before I spoke to Rae again.

Once I finally did, we decided that in the end, despite what had happened with Joey, we survived it. And that meant more to us than anything else.

Since then, we've managed to make our relationship more solid than ever. Together, we moved on and our once deep connection dug a hole even deeper.

Several weeks ago, Rae moved in with me and Joey, and so far things have been incredible.

Until life happened, again.

Life, the fickle thing, is a small reason as to why I'm here.

Trying to calm my nerves, I rub my palms together and sit forward. After taking a few moments to work some sentences through in my mind, I give the speech of a lifetime to Rae's father.

"To put it simply: I love your daughter. But if you're looking for the long version, here it is: She absolutely completes me. Last year when I met Rae, I was resigned to a life of single fatherhood. I had Joey and she was all I needed. Or at least that's what I thought at the time. But then this incredibly beautiful woman stepped foot into my shop and opened my eyes to what I was missing—her. Rae's wild. She's a little crazy, sarcastic as hell, a fighter, tough, and sweet all wrapped into one. Everything about her is amazing, even her flaws. Yes, she has them. Everyone does. And she's fantastic with Joey. *Holy hell* is she amazing with her. There's nothing that makes my heart more erratic than seeing them together," I tell Ted honestly. "I want to spend the rest of time with her because she's the most real thing I've ever had in my life."

Ted doesn't say anything; he only continues to stare at me. I start getting a little uncomfortable under his stare, but I don't back down. After another moment passes, I tell it to him straight.

"With all due respect, sir, nothing you say here today will deter me from asking your daughter to marry me. Nothing. And if she says 'yes,' I *am* going to marry her. Our love doesn't need the stamp of approval from someone who will never understand it like we do. This is all a formality."

A slow, almost sinister grin stretches across his face. "Brave. You're very brave, Hudson." He's looking at me like the fucking Cheshire Cat, and I'm man enough to admit I'm nervous as hell right now.

"And determined," Ted continues, sitting forward and mirroring my position. He's about a foot from me, holding my stare with a fierce one of his own. "Whether or not you need it, you have my blessing. I just wanted to hear you say that you loved my daughter enough to not let anyone tell you otherwise."

I expel a relieved breath and Rae's dad starts laughing. "Dammit, Mr. Kamden. You had me scared for a second."

"Couldn't resist screwing with you, son. And for the love of all holy things, call me Ted. I've already told you a million times."

"Sorry, sir. Shit. I mean Ted."

Ted gives a hearty laugh as he gets up to walk into the kitchen. "You want a beer?"

"No, thank you. I'm driving."

"Good answer."

I sink into the couch as he disappears to the other room. He said yes. *Fuck. Yeah.*

Now I just have to find the perfect way to propose. Low-key or large event? Simple or over the top? Audience or in private? How in the hell do people do this shit?

I'll be honest. I didn't *really* think this whole thing through. I only know that I want to marry Rae. Now. Tomorrow. Next month. Next year. Any damn day. I want her. I want forever with her.

We lost someone last month. The brother of my best friend was taken away in an unexpected accident. While we technically lost two people since Tucker is on the road, one of them still has the option to return. Tanner doesn't. While neither one of us was much a fan of him in life, his death has still taken a toll on us. So much so that we've spent the last several weeks discussing what would happen to Joey if I died, how we'd handle an emergency situation, and loss in general.

We're both accustomed to it—loss, that is. Rae's mother committed suicide when she was only seven, the same day Rae almost drowned, and my father passed away three years ago. Both of them were sudden. Each left everyone completely unprepared for the future without them. Neither one of us wants that for Joey.

I've never been one for legalities, but now, I want them. I want to know my future is bound to hers by a fancy contract. I want to know

I'm as legally hers as she is mine. And Joey. I definitely want the legalities for her.

Other than that, I don't *really* need them. In the deepest depths of my soul, I know. Rae is my forever. My tomorrow. My everything.

"I can hear the wheels spinning from the other room. Relax. You'll know when it's the right moment," Ted says as he walks back into the room, cold beer in hand. "Want to know how I proposed to Rae's mom?"

Ted must see the sadness in my eyes before I can hide it because he shakes his head. "It's okay, Hudson. We had many good years together before everything happened. I have some fond memories of Erin."

He takes a heavy, calming breath before starting his story. "We were young but wildly in love. We'd been together for two years and some change when we found out we were pregnant. You think we'd have been nervous since we were still living at home with our parents and barely scraping by, but we weren't. Our love was enough."

Rae's father sits back in his chair, eyes closed and chin tucked into his chest. I have this odd feeling he's realizing that in the end, their love *wasn't* enough. And it's breaking his heart all over again.

When he speaks, he stays in the same position, like he's trying to remember every last detail of what happened. "I had this whole huge night planned. We had just told her parents about the pregnancy, and they were surprisingly supportive of it. We went to dinner to celebrate—the fanciest restaurant I could afford. I had my timing perfected and everything was going according to plan. But then it wasn't. In the middle of our romantic dinner, she broke down in tears. And I mean sobbing. 'What are we going to do, Teddy?' she asked over and over again. I kept quiet and held her until her tears subsided, paid our bill, and walked her to the car. We drove down to Lake

Quannapowitt and walked to the shore, skipping stones for several minutes in silence. It was our thing. After about twenty minutes, she apologized for her breakdown, obviously embarrassed by what had happened. I knew it was all just the baby hormones. I was a kid, but I wasn't stupid. I understood how that stuff worked."

A small grin plays at Ted's lips, like he's watching a movie play in his head, detailing his happy memories with the woman who still owns his heart.

"I didn't respond to her apology right away. You want to guess what happened next?"

"I'm clueless, Ted. Knowing Rae, she'd probably start throwing stones at *me*. I have no idea if she has Erin's…spirit, but that'd be my guess."

Ted barks out a laugh, slapping his knee. "Damn. My baby girl is much more like her mother than she's ever realized."

"Nailed it, huh?"

"Oh, yes. That's exactly what she did. After I finally got her calmed down, I grabbed her face between my hands and kissed her senseless. I said, 'Erin, you're insane. You make me insane. But I love you all the same. We'll be fine. We'll *make* it fine. We have to. It's what we do. Now, put your crazy away for a minute, okay? I have something important to ask you.' And that was it. I asked her. Nothing fancy. It was just my heart, Hudson. I laid it out there plain and simple for her. Just follow your heart, kid. It's always right."

"Hudson? Is that you?"

"Hey, babe!" I shout, walking through the front door, following the sound of Rae's sweet voice to the kitchen.

Flour. That's all I can see. It looks like winter blew through and we left all the windows open. Mounds and mounds of snow-like powder sit on the floor and every square inch of counter space. I can already tell this isn't going to turn out how she planned.

"Um, what are you doing?" I ask as she's elbow deep in dough.

"Making chocolate chip cookies," she says, not breaking eye contact with what her hands are doing. She's concentrating so hard her tongue is poking out and her brows are furrowed. "There's a batch over there and one in the oven. I just need to make one more after this and I'm done."

"Mind if I try one?"

She nods. "Go for it."

I barely contain my laughter when I stop in front of her plate of cookies. Pointing to the cookies, I ask, "These them?"

Rae glances up to see where I'm pointing. "Yep. They look a little flat. Not sure what happened, but they still look edible. The kids will never know."

A little flat would be an understatement. They are *completely* flat. And I have this feeling the cookies are not "edible."

I gingerly bring a cookie up to my nose, sniffing it just in case I can smell something off about them from the start. *Fine.* Cautiously, I take a bite. And then I promptly spit it right back out.

"Ugh! What is *that*?" I toss the atrocity back down on the plate, scraping at my tongue.

"What? What do you mean?" Rae hollers, rushing over to the table and pushing me out of the way. "They look fine! Flat, but fine." She lifts my abandoned cookie and takes a huge bite. That too finds its way back onto the table. "Gross!"

Rae rushes to the sink, gulping water straight from the faucet. She wipes her mouth and runs over to her cookbook, scanning the page with her finger to find where she messed up.

"Shit!" she huffs, slamming the book closed and tossing it across the counter. "I forgot the baking soda."

I cringe. "That's kind of important."

"And I put too much flour in there," she mumbles, crossing her arms over chest. She's pouting. My adult girlfriend is legit pouting. But I can't blame her. I'd be pouting too if I had just spent the last several hours making cookies only to find out they taste like complete shit.

Wait. Why is she doing this again? She can't cook for shit, so I'm curious as to why she even tried baking in the first place.

"Why did you say you were making cookies?"

"For Joey's bake sale for her summer softball league. Since it's not school sponsored, they could be homemade, so I decided to try making them. But clearly I suck. I'm terrible at this domestic stuff, Hudson!"

I can't help it—I laugh. Hard. "Why are you doing this the hard way, then? Break and bake, babe. Break and bake. That's how I do it."

She throws her hands up in defeat. "See? Even you're better than I am and you suck too! I quit. Let's just order a pizza and pretend I made that from scratch too."

"Deal. Now go get the broom. We've got some cleaning up to do."

Rae marches away, muttering to herself the whole time. A very tiny part of me feels bad for her, but this is just too rich. She looked so proud of herself and so sure, only to forget the most important ingredient. Poor Rae.

"Here. You sweep, I'll swipe," she says, handing me the broom. "How'd everything go at the shop?"

The shop? I wasn't at the shop.

"I wasn't…" I start, barely catching myself and nearly blowing my cover. "I wasn't sure I'd ever get out of there."

"Sucks you had to go in, but I'm glad I've got you back now. It seems every week you're piled with paperwork. Guess that just means more cash flow and more money for us to spend on not-so-home-cooked meals."

I give her a distracted laugh and continue sweeping up her mess, the guilt of my lie pressing down on my shoulders like a damn boulder.

Yes, I've been lying to Rae. For weeks now, actually. Hell, even months.

You see, after Rae found out her father had been lying to her about her mother's condition and what really happened out in that blustery ocean when she was seven, she halted all communication with her father. On one hand, I understand it all. On the other, it breaks my heart. I'm certain it doesn't break mine as much as it does Rae's, considering she was extremely close with Ted, but it still hurts. It hurts to see Rae lose such a strong relationship with her dad, and it hurts to see the sadness lurking behind her eyes when someone mentions him.

While my heart may be sad for Rae, it hurts even more for Ted. Being a father myself, I understand exactly why he did what he did. And it's not like he outright lied; he just allowed Rae to believe whatever was going to make her feel safe. I'd do the same for Joey in a heartbeat.

So, yes, watching the woman I love live in such emotional pain is tough. Watching her father lose not only his wife, but also his daughter who he fought so hard to keep alive, is even worse.

To make up for the love Rae is incapable of showing her father right now, once a week I visit with him in her place. We talk, catch some of whatever game is on, and most importantly, we laugh together. Vital because Ted is lacking in that department since his big lie blew up in his face.

Let's just hope when the time comes to tell Rae what I've been doing, mine doesn't do the same thing.

I give her a wink and reply, "Someone's gotta pay for the food you burn."

"One time, Hudson! One time."

"Today, maybe."

Did you know flour tastes like shit? It's true. How do I know? I'm tasting it right now because Rae just blew a whole pile straight into my face.

Wiping off the disgusting powder, I launch at her, tackling her to the ground instantly. I roll over until she's pinned under me, kicking and screaming the entire time. Trapping her arms above her head with one hand, I run my fingertips down her overly ticklish sides. Her giggles and squirms are instant.

"I'm sorry, I'm sorry!" Rae pants, attempting to hold down her laughter.

"Nope, not good enough."

"I love you?"

"Closer…" I say, dropping my head next to hers and grazing my lips along her ear. Her giggles turn to soft moans and her squirms turn into more concentrated movements, her body rubbing against mine in sinful ways.

"You're the most amazing man in the whole wide world?"

"I know, darlin', I know," I tease. "Flattery will get you everywhere with me." I give her a quick peck directly below her earlobe before whispering, "But that's not what I want to hear."

I use the soft pressure of my lips mixed with day-old stubble to seduce the words out of her. I gingerly run them down her neck to her collarbone, begging the words to fall from her lips.

I know it's going to work when Rae's breaths become harsh like she's just finished scaling a mountain—which she kind of has since the two words I want to hear are about as strenuous for her to admit as the physical intensity of a climb.

While they are her least favorite words, they are far from mine.

She huffs, a mixture of irritation and sexual frustration. "Fine. I'll say it."

"Good. I knew you'd—"

"On one condition," she interrupts.

Lifting my head, I narrow my eyes at her. "You are in no position to negotiate."

"Oh, but I am, Hudson. You see, you're lying on top of me, attempting to rile me up—and it's working. But you've forgotten that your eight-year-old daughter is upstairs right now and can come down at any moment. That means your, ahem, excitement over our current position could be your downfall."

It's my turn to huff. "What do you want."

Nope, not even phrasing that as a question. Little sneak.

"*You* have to make the break and bakes because I'll probably burn the entire house down trying to do so."

Laughter rumbles in my chest. "You're exhausting."

Rae reaches up and nuzzles her nose against mine, lingering only seconds to graze her lips over my own. "But you love me anyway."

"Just a wee little bit."

She captures my mouth fully with hers. Her hands slip from my gentle grasp, going straight for my head, holding me to her like her life depends on it. I kiss her back with equal want, running my tongue across her lips, begging her to allow access. She does, but only briefly.

The heat we create together in these short stolen seconds is so overwhelming that I swear I smell smoke.

Shit!

"The cookies!" I yell, prying my lips from Rae's and jumping into action like a madman.

I move to the stove to rescue her crispy not-so-master-masterpieces as she rushes to open the back door and windows before the smoke alarms start sounding and send Joey into a panic.

Joe must hear the commotion because it's not even a minute later when she comes bounding down the stairs and straight into the kitchen. "What's happened? Is everything okay? Are we all going to die?" she asks, her eyes wide with fear and curiosity.

I mentally cringe but don't stop my movements.

That's another side effect of losing someone—children become consumed with the idea of death. They become aware, afraid, intrigued, confused. This technically isn't Joey's first encounter with the depressing event, but it *is* the first one that's happened since she's come to an age where she understands what occurs in the world around her. She knew my father when he passed. However, explaining it to her then was easier. She's had the last several years to come to terms with him never coming back. Tanner's death is still fresh and has her scared. She's panicked that those she loves will be ripped from her at any moment. Most of the adults I know may not have liked Tanner, because the dude was a total ass, but I can't deny the way he was always patient, kind, and loving to my daughter. I respect him for that more than anything.

"No one is dying, Joey. We're all fine. I promise," I reassure her, fanning the cookies with the oven mitt.

"Oh," she says. I can hear the worry leave her voice. "Rae, did you burn things again? Dad isn't a good cook either, but he doesn't burn things."

I swear Rae's word vomit has rubbed off on everyone around her because what Joey just said was exactly something Rae would say.

I snicker. "Always looking out for your old man. I appreciate it, kiddo."

"Hudson!" Rae scolds. She turns to Joey and says, "I may have baked your cookies for a few minutes too long. But your dad is going to make some more. Right, dear?"

Raising a brow at Rae, I challenge, "I don't know. Am I?"

I swear I can *hear* her roll her eyes at me. "You're right. I'm a terrible cook and I burn everything. Happy?"

"Finally! She admits it!"

She looks to Joey for help. "You just gonna let him be mean to me?"

Joey shrugs. "I know you said us girls were supposed to stick together when it came to dad being right, but…" she pauses, drawing the word out dramatically. "You do burn a lot of things."

"BURN! Just like your cookies!"

The look on Rae's face says I'm definitely in trouble for that little outburst.

Totally worth being in the doghouse.

Chapter Two

HUDSON

"You dragged me out on my one day off to go to the fucking mall? Dick move, Hudson."

"Shut up, you baby. I only invited you because Tucker isn't here," I tell my unhappy companion, and second best friend, Gaige.

"Gee. I feel *so* welcomed."

"Well if you weren't such a tool…"

"Hey! I'm the asshole, not a tool. Don't be mean."

I shoot him a look. "Really? You're okay with being called an asshole but not a tool?"

"Asshole just sounds so much more affectionate."

"You're so weird," I mutter. "Now, come on, *asshole.* We have several stores to look at."

Unusual for him, Gaige doesn't shut up as I navigate through the crowded mall. I forgot it was back-to-school season. The place is crawling with rambunctious teens. They're amusing and obnoxious all at the same time. I dread the day Joey turns into a teenager.

A teenager? Damn. That's only five years away. I'll be thirty by that point and probably feel about forty with the way my life has been on the fast-track since she was born.

But, if all goes as planned, I'll at least be settled down with the love of my life, a great house, thriving business, and Joey. Not exactly how I pictured some of my prime bachelor days but somehow exactly what I've always wanted.

"What are we getting here, anyway? It's not anyone's birthday, so I know you're not getting a gift. And you don't love me enough to randomly buy me presents, so that must mean you're…" He trails off as I steer us closer to the first jewelry store on my list.

When I realize he's not following me anymore, I stop my pursuit of shiny objects. I spin around to find Gaige frozen, his mouth hanging open in the middle of the packed shopping center. Suppressing a sigh, I walk back toward him.

"What."

"No fucking way," he says, shocked. "You're gonna propose."

I shift uncomfortably at the way he says it. He sounds awed. And his stare is starting to make me feel weird too. He's looking at me like I'm that damn three-headed dog from Harry Potter or some shit. I don't know whether that's good or bad. Not that I should base whether or not I'm going to propose on what Gaige thinks, but he's been in my life for a long damn time. I value his opinion above all others'. Well, except Tuck's and Rae's.

A grin transforms his naturally neutral expression to one of pure joy. "I'm so fucking happy for you, dude."

Blowing out a relieved breath, I say, "Thanks. That means a lot. But don't fucking tell anyone, okay? I haven't even told Tucker yet."

"You mean *I'm* the first to know?" Hand to God, the smile on his face resembles that of a kid's after they've just received the best gift ever.

"Calm yourself, dude. I don't like you *that* much."

"Liar," he says quickly. "You don't just keep me around for my good looks. You so love me, dude. We all know this already. What we don't know is why you haven't told Tucker. Or did you use your weird 'I see you' bullshit to communicate it long-distance or telepathically or some creepy shit like that?"

"You're just jealous *we* don't have a special saying."

"Obviously," he responds in mock seriousness. "But really, why not tell him? This is big."

"It's only big if she says yes."

"That's what she said. Nailed it!" Gaige shouts.

"Why? Why do I think going out in public with you is a good idea?"

"You don't. Now, back to Tucker."

I give a noncommittal shrug. "I don't know. He's on the road and I know he needs this time to separate himself from his life here. Plus, this is something I only recently started thinking about."

He creases his brows briefly before his face settles again. "Tanner," is all he says.

Gaige may be overly sarcastic and sometimes come off as an arrogant asshole, but he's the most observant person I've ever met. He just seems to know things and can read situations in seconds. And like usual, he's right on the money.

"Yes and no. I mean, it's not *only* because of that but also because I love her, ya know? She's just it for me. Why wait?"

"Can I say something?"

"If you're gonna be a dick, no. If you're going to say sweet things to me to try and get into my pants, it's still a no. I'm taken, Gaige."

"Well then I'm all out of things to say."

I snort. "Come on, you fuckin' weirdo. Let's go do this shit."

A bust.

That's what our trip to the mall was. Everything was too shiny, not perfect enough, or just plain ugly. Nothing felt…right.

"We suck at this shit, man," I complain to Gaige as we're walking back out the sliding doors.

"No, *you* suck. I know exactly what you need to get Rae."

I furrow my brow. "How the hell do you know what to get her when *I'm* the one dating her?"

"Because I'm the handsome, quiet, observant one that only engages in conversation when I can add in my unique sarcastic charm. I tend to pay attention and notice shit that others don't. Duh."

"How did I ever miss that," I deadpan. "So what is it that I apparently need to get her?"

"Simple. You need modest. No huge rock, no fancy setting. An elegant, simple band is perfect."

It doesn't take me long to know he's right. I kind of hate how he knew that and I didn't, but I'm also thankful one of us is smart.

"Can I confess something?" I say over the roof of my car.

Gaige points down to the door. "Want to unlock it? I think I felt a raindrop, and I can't mess up my hair."

On an eye roll, I unlock the car and we climb inside.

"I've been visiting Rae's dad."

"And signing your death wish," Gaige replies quickly.

I don't get even a little upset at his words, because I know he's right. Rae's going to be beyond pissed when she finds out. As wrong as it is, there's a small part of me that hopes to use our upcoming engagement as a distraction. It's not why I'm proposing, but I still hope it helps to fend her off a little. She can be a little unforgiving when she's angry.

Hence her not speaking to her father since she discovered the nightmares that have haunted her all these years weren't just nightmares; they were memories. Granted, it's a legit reason to stop talking to someone, especially since that was something very real and very tragic. But she hasn't even tried to see it from his point of view at all. And I guess she wouldn't because she's never been a father. She doesn't understand what it's like to want to protect your daughter with absolutely everything you have—no matter what it costs.

"I know she's gonna be pissed. I just hope she can see why I've been visiting him."

"And why's that?"

"Because she won't."

Gaige doesn't reply right away. The car is filled with the sounds of the seat belts zipping over us and clicking into place, the engine turning over, and Transit spilling from the speakers. We drive like this for several miles, and the distractions of the road and the music are welcome.

"I think you're doing the right thing." He says it so softly I almost don't hear him.

I turn down the radio and glance over at him. He's staring out the window. Most would think he's being dramatic, but I don't. No, this is Gaige. He's quiet, reserved, sarcastic, and thoughtful. He doesn't give his opinion often, but when he does, you better shut the hell up and listen to it because it's usually fucking gold that comes out of his mouth.

"I think it's okay that you're visiting her dad. Someone has to tell him she's doing well. Someone needs to let him know she isn't broken. You're that person now."

"But you said it yourself, man. She's gonna be pissed when she finds out."

"Hell yeah she will be. But so would you. Back when you weren't speaking to your pops, if she'd have done the same thing, you'd have been upset too. But then you'd have gotten over it just like she will."

There's nothing more I want than for him to be right, because the thought of Rae being so pissed she'd break it off devastates me. She can't not be in my life. That's not possible.

"I sure as hell hope you're right, dude."

"I usually am," he says confidently.

Chapter Three

RAE

"Can we go swimming?"

Those four words send chills through my body. My chest constricts. I feel like an astronaut stuck in space without a helmet. It's hard to pull any air through my lungs, and it's only coming out of my mouth in harsh waves.

"Why are you purple? Rae? Rae!" Joey shouts, pulling on my arm hard enough to drag my attention her way.

Air moves through my lungs and I gasp, finally able to breathe again.

"You okay?"

I look down at Joey and nod slowly. "I think so. I just had a...a moment."

"Moments are fickle."

My head snaps toward her, shocked at the words that just came out of her mouth. For such a tiny little human, she sure is pretty damn smart. "That they are."

"So can we go swimming?" she asks again.

I'm more prepared this time and shake my head. "I don't think that's such a good idea. Maybe when your dad gets home we can."

"Ugh! But he won't be home until later. Why can't we go now?"

"Um...because I said so?"

Her shoulders slump and she flings herself onto the sofa beside me. "Fine."

She looks so sad that I *almost* give in, but I stand my ground. I'm supposed to be a responsible adult now. I can't continue to give in every time she gives me those extremely convincing puppy dog eyes or pushes out her bottom lip. I've been very good at not giving in these last few months, especially considering how much I gave in when Hudson and I first started dating. Anything she wanted was hers. Ice cream? You got it! Pudding? Sure thing! A new book? Of course! Going swimming in the ocean while I have a freaky flashback thing and you nearly drown? Yep, that too.

So, no, she most definitely cannot go swimming on my watch. Even if it is in the neighborhood swimming pool. It's not happening.

"I have an idea. Why don't we go take your dad some lunch at work? That way we'll get out of the house and get to visit him some. How's that sound?"

"Fine."

Ah, the joys of mood swings and not getting your way.

"Good. Up. Let's make him something tasty," I tell her, pushing myself off the sofa and heading to the kitchen.

"How about we just order him something? That way we know it's not going to be burned."

I do my best to smother a laugh. "You're so your father's

kid."

I don't have to be looking at her to know she just rolled her eyes. "Obviously."

Boom. Boom. BOOM!

I pound on the doors to Jacked Up for the third time. The result is the same—no answer. And I don't see Hudson's car. I want to believe he's just stepped out for lunch, but I have this feeling he was never here at all.

I don't know whether or not the fact that he's obviously lied to me hurts more or the fact that he felt the need to do it in the first place.

"I... I don't think he's here," Joey whispers, picking up on my frustration.

The last thing I want is for her to be upset. "Ya know, maybe he just stepped out for some lunch. We *are* surprising him, so he wasn't expecting us. I'm sure that's where he is."

"Yeah. I guess so."

"Want to go over to Maura's and have lunch there? I'm sure she'd love to see you."

She instantly perks up because this kid *loves* Maura. "Yes! Please!"

I teasingly narrow my eyes at her. "You're supposed to love me most."

Joey pats my arm. "It's okay. You're my fourth favorite."

"Fourth! You're killing me, kid."

She shrugs and skips—*skips*—back to the car.

The short ride to Maura's is silent. I'm a little nervous to see her. She's been going through a tough time since Tanner's death and

Tucker's leaving, so I'm not sure which version of her I'll be getting today. For Joey's sake, I hope it's the happy-go-lucky one.

I let Joey push the doorbell once we reach Maura's apartment. We're immediately greeted by a tall, tanned, complete and total stud. No matter how many times I've been here in the last couple weeks, it still surprises me every single time Maura's new roommate opens the door.

"Hey, Rae, Joe. How are you beautiful ladies today?" Dallas says, moving aside and waving us in.

"G-good," Joey stutters. I want to laugh because I know her stuttering is a sign of nervousness. She's completely smitten with Dallas. She thinks he's "so cute."

"We're good. Maura here?"

"Babygirl! You've got company," he shouts. Then he bends down and whispers, "Today's a rough day. I'm glad you stopped by."

I give him a small smile and flick my eyes to Joey, silently asking him to keep her occupied while I go wrangle Maura out of bed.

"Hey, Joe, wanna go see who can eat the most ice cream in five minutes?"

This time I give him an *Are you fucking serious?* look, because really? Ice cream eating contest? He shrugs and ushers her off to start a brain freeze war.

I quietly make my way down the hall and briefly knock on Maura's door before letting myself in. Seeing her curled up in bed just blankly staring at the door causes my heart to hitch. I hate seeing my best friend hurting like this. The worst part is that she's not hurting in the traditional sense. I wish she'd cry or scream or break down. She does none of those things. Instead she retreats into her head and stays silent for days at a time. It's near impossible to get through to her when she gets like this. But I always try.

"Hey," I say softly. "How are you?"

She doesn't say anything. But she does scoot over, inviting me to come sit next to her. So I do.

"Joey's here." It's barely noticeable, but I can see a small smile touch her lips. "She's having an ice cream eating contest with Dallas. I'm not sure I like him anymore."

Her eyes finally leave the door and she looks at me.

"I do," she croaks out. "He's so damn good to me, Rae. I had a freak-out last night. He talked me down."

She's letting off wave after wave of sadness. I want to wrap her up and keep her safe from all this heartache, but I can't. She needs to feel it or she'll never be able to work through it. So all I can do it sit here with her. "Good. I'm glad you have him here."

"I miss him."

I don't need to ask who she's talking about.

"I know. I do too."

She blows out a breath, and I watch as she musters up the courage she needs to push through the day. It's slow, but eventually she's in a place where I know she'll be okay.

"So, what's up with you?"

"Hudson's not where he says he is."

Her eyebrows shoot up instantly. "Where is he, then?"

I shrug. "No clue. He's been going into the office a lot on Sundays, so Joey and I tried taking him some lunch today only to find the shop completely empty and no sign of his car."

"Come on. Say it, Rae."

She knows me way too well.

"What the fuck does it mean, Maura? I didn't think much of it before, but the fact that he lied about where he was going today makes me think he's been lying this entire time. Why? And where in the hell is he going if not to Jacked Up?"

I hate saying all this out loud. I hate having these fears. Hudson doesn't deserve accusations that come with the questions I'm voicing. But I also don't deserve to be lied to.

"I'm sure—"

"There's an explanation. Yeah, I know," I interrupt her. "But there shouldn't have to be an explanation. We should be able to be completely honest with one another."

Maura sits up and mirrors my dejected posture. "True. But sometimes it's necessary, Rae. What if he's planning a sweet surprise? What if he just had to go run an errand? What if he went to lunch? I don't think the conclusions you're jumping to are fair."

They're not. I know I'm being a little crazy about this right now, but something about the situation makes me feel uneasy. I can't ignore it.

"I feel horrible saying this all out loud, Maura. You know I love that man with everything I have. But something feels off."

"You do know the only way to get to the bottom of this, right?"

"Hold him down and feed him Veritaserum?"

"First of all, wow, you're a damn nerd. Second, that doesn't even exist in our Muggle world. Third, no."

"I'm a nerd? You're the one who knew I was referencing Harry Potter."

Maura scoffs. "Whatever. But my answer is still no. You need to just ask him about it. Give him the chance to explain. That's the only way it's going to be fair."

I sigh. "The Veritaserum sounded more fun."

She lets out a dry laugh. "It did, didn't it?"

"I hate when you're right."

"But you love *me*."

"That I do. Which is why I'm done watching you mope," I tell her, diverting the conversation back to her. "So, up. Let's go. We're leaving the bed today and we're going to go out there and eat ice cream until we can freeze all these shitty thoughts out of our heads."

"Oh, I love the way you think."

"And you love *me.*"

"That I do."

"Hey, babe. How was your day?" Hudson wraps his arms around me from behind, nuzzling my neck, nipping lightly at the spot he knows drives me insane. I don't want my body to react, but I can't help the way it automatically falls back into his embrace, molding to him perfectly.

I want to be angry with him for lying, I want to push him away. But as much as I want those things, I also want him to hold me closer, to be happy, to spin around and welcome him home with a kiss. Instead, I act naturally. And neutrally.

"Good," I tell him, rinsing off the plate I'm holding. "We went to visit Maura, had lunch with her and Dallas, who I'm growing quite fond of."

Hudson nips at my neck once more.

"I'm glad he's not into girls, because then I may have to act jealous."

I'd normally come back with a quick-witted comment, but I'm just not feeling the spar today. I can tell by the way his arms constrict around me that he notices.

"You gonna spill?"

Hudson drops his arms and takes a step back at the sound of

disbelief that involuntarily leaves my mouth. I wince because I know he doesn't deserve the cold shoulder I'm giving him. But I also don't deserve to be lied to.

Are you serious right now, Rae? You don't *know he lied! He could have just gone to lunch. Grow the fuck up already.*

I should listen to myself. I know I should. But I can't. Because my stupid fucking stomach is tied up in knots like a fucking sailor did that shit. Something's off. I can feel it.

"Right. Well, I'll leave you to your sulking, then. Let me know when you want to talk. I'm here for anything."

He sounds so sincere I almost cave. In fact, I spin around to do so. But as soon as I see his retreating back, I have the strongest urge to throw something at him. Which is entirely stupid because I don't know if he even did anything wrong.

I'm suddenly tired from the constant back and forth my brain is having with my stomach. Neither one of them will stop bickering. I feel sick.

I quickly finish the dishes, set out the menus for our weekly Sunday takeout, and head toward the stairs without saying a word to Hudson.

Relentless. That's one word someone could use to describe Hudson. I'm not even in our bedroom five minutes before he seeks me out.

"Babe, come on. Tell me what's wrong," he tries, closing our bedroom door and relaxing on the bed next to me but not touching me.

I hate that he's not touching me.

"You."

"Me, what?"

"You. You're what's wrong."

I swear I can hear the wheels turning in his head. "Why am I what's wrong?"

I don't answer for a long time. So long that I feel his breathing start to even out. So long that I'm certain the dark, quiet room has nearly lulled him to sleep.

"We tried to bring you lunch today," I whisper.

Silence. I'm met with silence. But I know he heard me, and I know he's awake now because he shifts a little. I feel an arm snake around my waist and I'm being pulled into his warmth. I relax instantly. Being in his arms will always relax me. No matter how mad I am, no matter how annoying he is, no matter the bitchiness that's swallowing me whole, being touched by him is guaranteed to soothe me.

With my ass pressed against his dick, I can feel him growing hard. I push back on him, loving the feel of him against me. His hand finds my breast and gently cups it, taking my hardened nipple between his thumb and forefinger. I moan as he rolls it between them, applying just the right amount of pressure. Everything with Hudson is just the right amount.

Soft lips trace a path from my shoulder to my neck. Light nips are quickly soothed by small licks, and my entire body is on fire. I roll over and slam my mouth against Hudson's, pressing my front to his, throwing a leg over him so his erection fits snuggly between my legs. He rolls us over so he's on top, pinning me to the bed, never once breaking our kiss. His tongue prods, making love to my mouth, saying the words he can't out loud. He knows I'm mad. I know I'm mad. Neither one of us cares right now.

We don't care as my hands find his shirt and he rips it over his head. We don't care as I unsnap his pants and draw down his zipper so he can kick his jeans away. Nor do we care when he strips away my clothes piece by piece. The moment all care in the entire world is thrown directly out the window is when he gently parts my legs and enters me with one quick thrust.

No words are spoken, no sounds are made. But the room is still loud, filled to the brim with our thoughts, our silent communication, our unspoken bond, our *love.* And the questions surrounding us and this moment are endless and tight and reaching out to grab at all the perfect moments we've ever had. Something is shifting.

And I'm not sure I like it.

Chapter Four

HUDSON

"Something happened last night, man."

My head snaps up at the grim tone of Gaige's voice.

"What's up?"

"I heard Tucker on the radio."

A smile takes over my face instantly and my chest swells with pride. *My best friend is on the fucking radio.* I wish I could say I helped him get there, but I didn't. I may have pushed him to finally follow his dreams, but nothing has carried that man more than his talent. And I'm beyond proud of him for that, so I'm a little thrown by Gaige's statement.

"Why is that a bad thing?"

"Because that means the fucker is honestly good and isn't coming back. Ever. I don't like that. He's a prick."

I chuckle because it's such a typical response coming from Gaige. When he gets uncomfortable with his emotions—pride in this case—he reverts back to the one thing he excels at: sarcasm. And insults, apparently. So let's just go ahead and make that two things.

"You know you're proud as hell," I say, focusing back on my laptop because I'm horribly behind on work.

"Whatever," he mumbles as he shuffles into the room, takes a seat, and props his shoes up on my desk. "You know you miss him."

"True."

"You want him to go and be big and famous, don't you?"

"Mhmm."

"And you want him to go off and leave us all behind and never, ever talk to us again?"

"Yep."

"You're also not listening to a single thing I'm saying right now. Hudson, can I have a raise? How's two dollars more an hour sound?"

"Sounds like you're not getting a raise," I tell him, closing my laptop and knocking his dirty boots off my desk. "You've sufficiently distracted me. Now what do you want?"

"Nothing, man. Just having an off day."

I lean back in my chair and fold my hands behind my head. "I feel you."

"Oh, shit," he says, leaning forward and resting his elbows on his knees. "Trouble in your disturbingly perfect paradise?"

I hate that everyone thinks Rae and I don't have problems. I guess in reality they aren't that big of a deal, but it's not like we don't ever fight or disagree on things. We do. All the damn time. She's stubborn as shit and a little crazy. I can be mean and short-tempered on occasions. Don't get me wrong, I know those aren't huge issues, but for us, that's enough. We struggle just like every couple. Our difference is that we choose not to. We don't let the little shit bother us. We work through it. There's no other option for us.

Except for last night. I got home after seeing her dad and could tell right away that something was wrong. I don't know what tipped me off to her mood. It could have easily been her rigid shoulders or her quiet greeting or the fact that she was scrubbing the dishes like they'd been sitting in dog shit for the last six months. Then she did something that sent the *maybe something is up with Rae* meter off the charts—she dodged me. An upstairs-lights-out-no-goodnight dodge. Then I found out what was wrong with her. She knows I lied to her about working yesterday. I also know that she's now questioning everything. Especially since after she gave me the perfect opportunity to come clean to her, I did something I never do either.

I dodged *her.*

Or at least her question. Or statement, rather. Then I seduced her, let her fall all over me. Whatever. We didn't talk about it. Just moved on, had our dinner, and ignored it. And this morning? Yep. Ignored it then as well. So for the first time in a very long time, something is majorly off with our relationship.

And it's all my fault.

"You okay?" Gaige prods.

"I think I've royally fucked up."

"I'm sure you have."

I give him an incredulous look for that comment.

"What? It was bound to happen," he defends. "After all the bliss, there's going to be a storm. The weather isn't perfect all the time, especially not around these parts. When you want summer, you get winter. When you want spring, you get all the damn rain Mother Nature can throw at you. There's no happy medium. This seems like autumn to me."

Did he just compare my relationship to the fucking weather, to the seasons? And did he just make complete and total sense? Yes, yes he did.

"I know." He taps the side of his head. "I'm a genius."

"Or entirely insane."

"It's a fine line, so who's the real winner?"

I can't help but laugh at him. He always spins things to his favor. "Your confidence in yourself is always so inspiring, Gaige."

"You're welcome," he says automatically. "But do enlighten me as to how you've royally fucked up. I'm curious as to how the great Hudson can do that. I mean other than sneaking around and visiting her dad. Which I still believe she'll eventually forgive you for."

"Eventually?"

He shrugs. "I'm nothing if not hopeful."

"Something like that," I mutter.

"Well? Spill, fucker. Some of us have shit to do."

I let out an irritated sigh because *he's* the one who barged in here to bother *me*.

"I dodged her, man. Last night. She basically caught me lying to her about working yesterday, and I fucking dodged her. Sidestepped her like I was on a damn football field. And she didn't even try to block me. She just let me pass and I scored. Only I feel like I've cheated us both by doing so."

He doesn't say anything, just narrows his eyes. And then the silence continues until I'm squirming in my chair.

"What," I grit out.

"You're telling me that you used sex as a distraction? You, Hudson Tamell, Mr. Perfect, did that? Wow. I feel like a fucking saint right about now."

"What makes you feel so holy?"

"Even I haven't done that. I mean I'm an asshole and all, but that's low, man. Like, Hell level low."

"I'll be sure to save you a seat down there."

"You're too good to me." He pauses to let me know he's about to get serious. "Listen, man, it's gonna be okay. Yeah, she gave you an excellent opportunity to fess up to the sneaking around—I'm not sure why you didn't do just that—and you completely blew it. But I think it'll be okay in the end."

I don't miss the "think" part of his sentence. Nor do I miss him pointing out that I didn't fess up.

Honestly, I'm not sure why I didn't either. I'm not a fan of confrontation and I know this is going to lead to an argument eventually. But I also don't think Rae's ready to know just yet. I'm not sure how she's going to handle it and that terrifies me. I'm scared of losing her.

Fuck. I'm scared of losing her. That right there is the reason I'm still hiding it, why I didn't confess to sneaking around. I know this could be the thing that breaks her, the thing that tears her away from me. I don't want that.

No, I want her to understand why I've been visiting Ted, why I'm so insistent on maintaining some sort of connection between the two. I know firsthand what it's like to lose a father. I know how it feels to have your entire relationship just vanish. Right now they still have that thread connecting them. Sure, Rae's pissed. But she's not completely closed off. Not yet. And I'm not going to let her get to that point. No matter the stakes in our relationship.

"Your head's spinning, huh?" Gaige interrupts my thoughts.

"Hell yeah. I'm just so...conflicted. I want everything for her, but I don't want to lose her."

He sighs, and it's a long, drawn out one. I don't think I like those kinds of sighs. "Are you ready to risk it though?"

"I am." My response is automatic because it's damn true. Because the truth is, she needs that relationship with her father far more than she needs me.

"Goddamn. You are one selfless man."

I wish I wasn't, though. I wish just this one time that I could be selfish. But when it comes to Rae, I could never be. I suppose I should consider that a blessing and not a curse.

In a hardly seen moment of seriousness, Gaige says, "I'm in awe of you, man. You were dealt some rather fucked up cards in life at a young age, but you didn't let that get you down. You became a way better man for it, and I'm honored to call you my friend."

I do my best to choke back the emotions begging to be let out. I don't think I can explain to him how good that felt to hear. I know this is silly, but there are so many days when I worry about whether or not I'm doing a good job as a dad. I think most people worry about those things, but based on where I am in life right now, I don't feel like I have a reason to do that. But…I do. I'm just glad hard work is something others can see. It's nice to feel like I'm helping make a difference somehow, someway.

"Uh, thanks, man," I tell him, my throat thick from holding in how I feel.

He shrugs. "Yeah, whatever."

I immediately bark out a laugh, because damn, only Gaige could spit out some sweet, meaningful shit like that and then follow it up with two words and a shrug to show his indifference. The best part is that he means it. He doesn't care or ever apologize for what he says. Or doesn't say. He's a good dude.

"Anyway, I guess I'm going to get back to work. Someone's gotta keep this place afloat when Rae kills you in your sleep for being a total shithead."

I give him a short, humorless laugh. "Wow. Thanks for the pep talk. I feel *so* much better now."

"Anytime," he says somberly as he pushes himself from his chair and makes his way to the door.

Every time I get done talking with Gaige, I always feel a

little...confused. He makes sense—always does—but he also has this way of making you feel...thoughtful. It's like he forces everyone to be the outsider he always claims to be, makes people step back and really look at things from a different angle.

"Hudson?" His voice pulls me from my thoughts. I glance up to find him still standing in the doorway, looking back at me. I raise an eyebrow and he continues. "For what it's worth, I think you're doing the right thing. And even going about it in the right way. You're a smart man, but Rae's an even smarter woman. She's going to figure it out eventually and shit's going to implode on you. But that's okay. You're an expert at taking a crap situation and making it pretty damn decent. You'll be fine."

He doesn't give me a chance to respond before he walks out the door. I smile to myself because even though I've always felt like I've chosen some excellent people to call friends, Gaige just completely reaffirmed my belief in that. So, I'm going take what he's said and attempt to stop worrying about it.

Attempt.

My door gets pushed open twenty minutes into me finally getting back into my groove after lunch. I've been a mess all morning. My attempt to try to focus and not think about Rae and how I *might* be fucking everything up royally is failing. Horribly. All I can focus on is how this is going to end. And I'm so scared it's not going to go the way I want it to go.

Actually, I *know* it's not.

"Knock, knock."

"Hey. Come on in, babe," I say to Rae, getting up from behind my desk and going to hug her. I feel a slight twinge in my chest as she puts her head down and goes the complete opposite direction of me. Intentionally.

I hate that there's this hole between us. It's dark and black and it's sucking us both into a dance that I don't want to dance. While we're both dancing, we're not dancing *together*. It's the worst dance I've ever danced. And I suck at dancing.

"We need to talk." She heads straight to the two chairs sitting opposite my desk.

I sigh loudly, closing the door and following her lead. She doesn't look at me when I sit down. She doesn't return my touch when I reach out and brush my finger across the back of her hands that are braced on her knees, her knuckles turning white from her strong grip. She just sits there, staring straight ahead.

"Rae..."

She flinches, like my saying her name has caused her physical pain. That twinge I felt in my heart earlier has now turned into a constant, dull ache. I don't like this.

"You're hiding something."

It's not a question. I hate it when she doesn't ask questions and just states things. It makes my deceiving her seem more real.

Swallowing the lump of lies in my throat that are clawing their way to the tip of my tongue, I say, "I am."

Chapter Five

RAE

I am. He is.

My eyes are instantly on fire. Tears want to fall. No, not fall. They want to create a river. They want to fill the room, spill out into the hallways, and run all the way through town. Because right now, I'm hurting. *Everything* is hurting. Hudson's been lying to me.

Lying. To me. His girlfriend. For God knows how long. *I need to know how long.* Wait. I don't want to know the answer to that. *Yes, I do.* Wait. *No. No, I don't.*

"How long?" I find myself saying.

I watch him slowly swallow the lies that want to spill out of his mouth. Again.

"A while."

"How long is a while?"

"Long enough."

His eyes dart across the room and I don't like that he won't look at me. I don't like that his hands are shaking. I don't like *this.* I feel…lost. Confused. Unsure. I want to know what exactly he's been lying about, but I'm suddenly afraid to ask.

"What?"

"Huh?"

I swallow the accusations that want to jump out of my mouth, the proof I have that he wasn't at work yesterday when he said he was. Instead, I play it safe, sticking with the only question I can muster right now.

"What…what are you lying about?"

He pales, his expression falling from one of confusion to one of panic. He's scared. Worried. I just don't know about what.

"I…" He starts. "I'm…uh…"

My patience is wearing thin. Whatever is going on, I just want to know about it. I want that other shoe to drop. I want to know the truth.

"It's a simple question, Hudson. What have you been hiding from me?"

He lifts his hand to the back of his neck, the muscles in his arm bulging from how tight he's squeezing. He's panicking. Then *I'm* panicking because what. The. Hell? *I'm* the one who came in here to get the truth from him, the one who's pushing him for info. So why am I now having second thoughts? Is it because I know something's wrong? Because I feel like there's this anchor unrelentingly dragging us into a choppy sea.

"Hudson."

He opens his mouth again only to close it just as quickly. And then, Hudson drops to one knee. *Apparently I don't need to ask again.*

Panic claws at me. Is he going to propose? I mean, normally that's what one does when they drop to one knee. That or they're tying their shoe. *Yes!* He's just tying his shoe, he's not proposing. He. Is. Not. Proposing.

Don't be stupid, Rae. He's fucking proposing. Holy shit! I'm…he's…marriage. Together. Forever. Not that I haven't already planned to have that with Hudson, but marriage makes it all so much more real. Permanent. I want that. I want to marry him.

"Rae…I…," he starts. He's making eye contact, but it's not *real* eye contact. It doesn't feel like *our* eye contact, that special thing we share where I swear we can see into each other's souls.

My momentary high is gone in a flash. Something feels off.

"I love you. *So* much. You *know* that."

I don't like that he's stressing certain words. I feel like he's trying to convince me of something, convince me to say yes.

"Will you marry me? Please?"

Desperate. He sounds desperate and unsure. His voice is unsteady. I *need* him to be sure. He's looking at me with insecure eyes. Hudson isn't insecure. Flags fly up. *This feels wrong.* This isn't what I wanted in this moment. I wanted to feel secure in his question and in my answer. I don't. None of this is like it should be.

He's looking at me expectantly, and all I can feel is that stupid fucking anchor pulling at me, dragging me down to the depths of the sea. The waves are choppy. *Or maybe those are my breaths?* Because I know now what I'm going to say—no. And it's going to hurt us both. I don't know how it's going to change our relationship beyond today, but I know it'll change it. *This* will become our new anchor. This is what will weigh us down. But I *have* to do it. For us. For our future. We can't start something as important as this when it doesn't feel right.

"N-no," I say unsteadily.

"No?" I don't know whether his voice is uncertain or relieved.

"No, Hudson. I won't marry you. Something feels…off." I phrase my statement as an opportunity for him to say something, to come clean.

He doesn't. And my heart breaks even more.

"I…I have a ring. Just not here."

I stare at him, unsure of what to say, because a ring is the last fucking thing I care about right now.

"I'm, uh, going to head back home," I finally manage.

He doesn't reach out to stop me from leaving. I don't like that he doesn't reach out. I don't like that he hasn't asked again. I don't like that he's not begging me to marry him. That just proves to me even more that something isn't right.

"Rae."

I let my hand linger on the doorknob, turning around to face him. I raise a brow in question.

"Will you be there tonight? When I get home?"

"Will you be honest with me?"

His eyebrows scrunch together. "I have been honest, Rae. I *want* to marry you."

My feet move, and before I know it, I'm standing right in front of Hudson, close. He's staring down at me, his eyes clouded with confusion, pain, and anger.

"And I want to marry you too, Hudson. So badly. But I can't. Not until you've been honest with me…"

"I have been…"

"*Really* honest with me. You haven't been that. Something's off. We need to fix that before we can move forward."

He sighs and I feel his breath on my face. I want to inch closer to him. I want to press my lips to his, to kiss away this weirdness between us, to *feel* him. Hudson makes the first move, leaning forward, tilting his head just right. He lifts his hands and cradles my face. His lips hover over mine. He's hesitating too.

"Rae," he breathes.

This moment right here feels like the real deal. *This* feels normal, like what it's supposed to be like with Hudson. This is us floating rather than sinking. I love it when we float.

He dips his head lower, his lips brushing against mine in just the slightest. "Rae, I—"

"Knock, knock, boss," Liam, one of Hudson's employees, calls as he opens the door. "Oh, shit."

The spell is broken. Hudson and I take a step back from one another, putting back the distance that's been steadily growing between us.

Liam clears his throat. "Um…uh…sorry, man."

"It's fine, Liam. We were just finishing up our conversation," I say coolly.

I retreat to the door, rushing to make my escape, to get fresh air so I can clear my head. For a moment, just a split second, everything felt right again. And then reality crashed in and wrongness settled.

A hand curls around the door just as I'm about to pull it shut.

"Tonight?" Hudson asks.

Do I want to go home to him? Of course. Do I want to go home to a house full of awkwardness? No, not at all. But I need to. I need to face this. *We* need to face this. Tonight may give us an opportunity to talk about things, to open up a little further.

Hopefully.

This time, I don't look back at him. "I'll see you at home, Hudson."

I swear I hear a sigh of relief before he clicks the door shut behind me.

Chapter Six

HUDSON

I feel like an intruder in my own home. Every move I've made has been calculated, careful. I'm tiptoeing around our conversation from this afternoon, around the proposal. Correction—the shot-down proposal.

She said no. I mean, an extremely small part of me thought she would with everything that happened last night. But I honestly thought this, asking Rae to marry me, would make things better, not worse. I was very wrong. It's actually made things worse, if that was even possible. Then again, how stupid could I be for thinking a proposal was the way to fix what's wrong? Not that that's what I was doing. Well, not entirely. Actually, not mostly. Nope. Not at all. This was all because I fucking love Rae. Maybe the timing has something to do with why I picked today to do it, but that's not the reason I want to marry her.

But I'm also an asshole because she's right. I have to fess up to what's been going on with her dad. And now. Or else this is going to ruin us. Hell, it may even still be able to. But I *have* to get this off my chest.

"Daddy? Did you hear me?"

I turn to Joey. "Of course I did."

Lie. Lie lie lie. That seems to be all I do these days.

"Then can I?"

"Can you what?"

Joey scowls. I look to Rae for help, hoping like hell she was paying attention. She rolls her eyes and answers Joey's questions with a "yes."

"Thanks!" Joey shouts. Then she's pushing away from the table, dumping her plate in the sink, and running up the stairs all within five seconds.

"Don't run!" I yell after her. I glance over at Rae. "What is she doing?"

Rae stares at me blankly. "She just asked if she can be excused to go play on the Wii."

"Oh."

"Glad one of us was paying attention." She grabs her plate and mine, walking them to the sink and throwing off cold air in her retreat.

I stand and follow her, placing both of my hands on the counter on either side of her waist, caging her in so she can't run this time. She stiffens instantly. I hate that she stiffens.

Lowering my lips to her ear, I say, "We need to talk."

This time she shivers. I love that she shivers. It means *something* is still there between us. I need so badly for something to still be there. I don't want distance between us anymore.

She spins around, but I refuse to back up in the slightest. We're standing so close that I can feel her chest brush against mine every time she breathes. And right now, that's a lot because her chest is rising and falling in rapid succession. From what, I'm not sure. But judging from the fire dancing behind her eyes right now, I think it's safe to say she's not very happy with me.

"*Now* you want to talk. Not this afternoon when I came to you asking for the truth? You want to do this *now*?"

"Hell yes I want to do this now. I shouldn't have to walk around my own damn house like I'm gonna run into a tripwire at any moment. That's not fair."

"Your lies aren't fair, Hudson."

Her words hit me like a fucking brick. I guess I deserved that though.

Sighing, I lean into her, needing to *feel* her. I rest my forehead against hers, our lips barely grazing. "Will you kiss me? Please?"

She sighs this time and I catch a tear rolling down the side of her cheek. "I hate that you even have to ask that."

"I hate asking it."

I notice she doesn't answer my question, but I don't care. I press my lips to hers. We don't move. We don't try for more. We just stand there, holding our lips together, taking this moment in. Then suddenly, we're *really* kissing. I don't know who reaches for whom first, but we're instantly wrapped up in one another. Within seconds, I have her up on the counter, her legs wrapped around me, writhing her tight, small body against mine. My cock is standing at attention, pressing into the heat between her legs. I hear a moan and I don't know who it came from.

Then I'm stumbling backwards, being pushed away, and Rae is crying. Hard.

"What the…?" I scrub a hand over my face and move back in to her, gathering her in my arms, squeezing her tightly, trying to take away all the hurt. "I'm sorry, Rae. I'm so fucking sorry."

"You…" She sniffles, wiping her cheeks on my shirt. The tears soaking through feel like fucking fire. "You can't fucking do that, Hudson. You can't just use kisses and sex to get out of this. It's too big. I don't know what you're hiding, but I can feel in my gut that it's a big one."

I hate this. I hate that I've been hurting her for God knows how long now. I wonder…

"How long have you felt this way?"

"Not long, really. Just a couple weeks. I've just noticed you've been working on the weekends a lot, but it doesn't ever feel like you've actually been working when you come home, ya know?" She gives a humorless laugh, pushing me off her again. "Of course you know. Because you *haven't* been working."

She looks at me, her eyes lit up with anger. She's fucking pissed and I don't blame her one bit.

It's time. I take a step back from her, letting us both have room to breathe.

"You're right. I have been hiding something from you."

"How long?" She repeats the same question from earlier today and I wonder why she keeps asking that.

"Why does it matter?"

"Because I want to know how long you've been dishonest with me. I *need* to know. Given my past, you should understand that."

I wince because this ties so much into her past, and I know that's what will be the real kicker here. *That's* what's going to get her.

"Since two months after the beach."

I can see it—she wants so badly to explode, to rage. But somehow, she manages to wrangle it all in and whisper, "Almost a year."

I inhale sharply at her words. Because fuck. It doesn't feel like that long. This feels so much worse than it did just moments ago.

"Rae, I…"

She holds her hand up to me, and I shut up instantly. "No. Stop. I don't want more lies, Hudson. I don't want excuses. I want the truth."

I gingerly take a step toward her, a little scared of how she's going to react to what I'm about to say. "I'm…I'm scared to tell you."

"*You're* scared? That's about the most bullshit thing you've ever said to me. You need to tell me. And now. Or you're going to run this relationship straight into the ground."

I don't budge, but instead direct my stare to the ground. I can feel her staring at me, willing me to speak. I don't. I just...stare.

"Please."

A shaky breath. A slight gasp. A quiver to my legs.

What I'm about to say is going to change our relationship in a big way, and I'm so much more terrified than I ever admitted before. I don't want to lose her. But that's the risk I took when I started this whole thing. That's the gamble I made when I decided to start seeing Ted on the weekends without her knowing. This is the moment it's all been leading up to, and I *have* to tell her. Now. Or she's right, I will run this relationship into the ground. I can't let that happen.

"I've been seeing someone because you won't."

Her brows furrow in confusion for a split second before pain seeps into her gaze. I know she's connected the dots the moment a strangled breath falls from her lips.

"Your father."

She explodes. "You what! You have got to be kidding me! After everything? After what he did? All this time you've been slinking around visiting him? Becoming his *friend*? What for?"

At this point, she's shaking and shouting and begging for air. She's panicking. I cross the room and lift her, placing her on the counter and grabbing her face in between my hands, trying to soothe her with my words.

"Breathe, sweetheart. Breathe. In, out. In, out. Stop shouting.

Joey's upstairs."

She stiffens. *Maybe terms of endearment aren't a good idea right now.*

I hear the crack of her hand across my face before I feel it. She gasps and I clench my jaw, grinding my teeth hard, reeling in the anger that I know is coming off me in waves right now.

I look at her and see how much she regrets slapping me. But I don't want her to regret it. I deserved it. *I fucking deserved it!*

"I deserved that for lying. But that's the only reason I deserved that." I squint at her when she opens her lips. She closes them, losing whatever argument she was just trying to cook up because she knows I deserved it too. "Now, do you want me to tell you why I've been seeing him?"

"Yes," she says automatically. "Just try to actually tell the truth this time."

Her words burn. It's like I stuck my hand into an open fire and the flames are slowly licking their way up my arm, going straight for my chest. The pain sinks in and I can feel the corners of my mouth tip down just the slightest.

"At first I understood your anger toward him. I got it on so many levels. He hid things from you practically your entire life, led you to believe the drowning was all a nightmare. Your being upset was one hundred percent justified." I pause, waiting for her to say something. She doesn't. "Rae, you wouldn't see him. You wouldn't answer his phone calls. Anytime he tried to reach out to you, you turned away from him. I've been on that end with my own father. I've been the one pushed away and I've done my fair share of pushing back. I hated it. Every single damn second, I hated it."

I close my eyes, thinking of my dad, Rocky. Of the fun we used to have together, of the summer trips to the beach, of the football games, and many games of hide and seek. And then I'm thinking of the summer everything went to shit, the summer I got Jess, my high school girlfriend, pregnant. At sixteen. I remember the fights and the screaming, the punches thrown, and the pain of being kicked out of my home right after I turned seventeen. I'm conjuring images of powering my way through school on no sleep from a crying baby, working endless nights and weekends to make ends meet for my little family, and how my father refused to help or see me for years. Then, I think of the day we first spoke again, the day everything changed for the better, the first sign of love from my dad in years and how whole I felt again. Until I wasn't. Because he was taken away from me again, and my entire world shifted when he died just three years ago.

When I open my eyes again, they sting from the tears I'm fighting so hard to hold back. I want to let them out, because I can do that with Rae. Or I used to be able to do that with her. Now, she feels closed off. I can tell from the way her jaw is screwed tight and eyes narrowed, waiting for me to continue.

"You don't get it until you lose it, Rae. You don't understand how much these things don't matter until you lose them. Your father is your best friend. He's the only parent you've ever had. You *need* him. You want him in your life and I can see that so much more than you can because my judgment isn't clouded by anger. For the past year I've watched you reach for your phone to call Ted on so many occasions. When you got your job, when we moved in together. Hell, even when you made your first pot of boxed mac 'n' cheese without turning the noodles to paste. I've watched you struggle. I'm tired of watching you struggle. You need him."

I can see her jaw ticking, practically feel the tension rolling through her body.

"*I* need *him*? I don't *need* anyone. Especially not someone who lied to me for twenty-two years of my life. Not someone who refuses to admit he was wrong in hiding the fact that my mother tried to drown me and then killed herself. I. Don't. Need. Him. And right now, Hudson, I don't need you stepping in and trying to play the knight in shining armor for me."

I don't say anything, because what's left to say?

"Let me get this straight." She huffs and crosses her arms over her chest. "You think that because you screwed up in your past with your father that you can suddenly butt into my—*my*—relationship with my father. And what, Hudson? What do you expect to come of this? What do you *think* is going to happen? That I'll just wake up one day and say all is forgiven because he's been talking to *you*? That's not how this works."

She pushes me away from her, hops off the counter, and begins pacing. I stay silent, watching the wheels spin in her head. I want to stop them, want to throw a wrench directly into them. But I don't. Because whatever she's thinking in there is probably the truth. Rae knows me well enough to be able to guess just exactly what's been going on.

She comes to a halt, spinning to face me, burning me with the fire in her eyes. "What have you told him?"

"What?"

"What have you fucking told him, Hudson? Everything? All that's been happening? All of our conversations? Our private fucking conversations!" She's yelling at this point, and I don't want Joey to hear any of this.

I laugh at myself because I'm such a fucking asshole. I had no problem just minutes ago with having her pinned against this counter, her legs wrapped around me, ready to carry her to our bedroom and fuck away this horrible day.

You're a dick, Hudson. A grade A dick.

"Keep your voice down. Please."

"What have you told him?" she repeats.

Sighing, I say, "Everything."

I feel like we're in one of those old western films where they square off in the middle of the street. A shootout. Only we're fighting with our words, with our feelings. Right now, I know I'm winning because the look on her face tells me I've shot her right in the heart with that one simple word. I don't want to win.

"Well, not *everything*. But enough."

"Why?" It comes out a broken whisper.

"Because he needs to know how you feel and someone had to tell him. You're an adult, Rae. Running from this isn't going to solve anything at all. You can't just keep ignoring him. You have to talk, you have to get it out. It's eating at you and you don't even realize it."

"It's not your place, Hudson. Not even a little bit."

"As the man who's madly in love with you, it's my place to see that you're happy. And you're not. I mean, you are, but you're not. Not really. Not when you're not talking with your best friend."

I have a point and she knows it. For the past year, she's had this…void. A hole, if you will. It's been lingering and growing by the day. I've continued to ignore it, ignore everything. It's been wearing on her. I can tell she's close to her breaking point, and I *have* to fucking fix it.

"This…this is big, Hudson. I-I don't know how to trust you now."

My entire body deflates at her words. That stings so much more than I thought it would. "I know." I clear my throat. "I knew that was coming. I thought I was prepared for that, but I realize now I was wrong."

"I…need out."

"Out?"

"Yes, out. I need to leave. *Now*."

"Leave?"

I sound like a fucking caveman, only able to mutter one-syllable words. Rae must agree because she shoots me a look.

"Yes, Hudson. Fucking leave. I need to get out of this house. I'm…I'm pissed. No, I'm *hurt.* I can't handle this right now. I…I need to go pack a bag."

She heads for the stairs and I immediately grab for her wrist.

"Wait." She pulls from my grasp, picking up her pace.

No. She can't leave like this.

"Goddammit, Rae. Just wait a fucking minute." My voice vibrates around the room loud enough to make her stop, but not turn around. "You can't just leave like this."

She heaves a sigh. "I can. And I'm going to. I need time, Hudson. I can't think in this house right now. I feel like I'm drowning." She looks over her shoulder, her eyes sad and pained. "And you're the one holding me under."

Chapter Seven

RAE

I wake up next to a sweaty, unfamiliar body. *Where am I?*

"You're at my apartment."

"Your apartment? This is *my* apartment, jackass."

I hear someone scoff. "No, *princess*, this is *our* apartment. Remember? I shared my B&J's with you. That means we share everything now."

"What? Are you—"

"B and fucking J's, Maura. All your secrets are mine now."

"Ohmygod. Why did I ever think it was okay to let you move in? You're insane!"

Laughing, I push the pillow off my head. "You're *both* insane." Looking at Maura, I say, "Sharing Ben and Jerry's is a privilege. You two are basically best friends now." Then I glance over at Dallas. "Fuck you for stealing my best friend."

"Sorry," Dallas says, looking anything but.

I grab my pillow and slap him with it. "Jackass."

"I can't believe we all fit in this bed last night," Dallas comments.

"With your fat ass, I'm surprised we did too."

Dallas doesn't even look hurt by Maura's comment. Instead, he smirks. "I do have a fantastic ass."

My best friend groans in mock frustration. "That's not even remotely what I said."

"Same difference."

His response is met with a pillow to the face. He immediately retaliates with not his, but *my* pillow. Naturally, this leads to a pillow fight between the two of them. I roll over, lying quietly in the middle, occasionally getting slapped across the ass with a pillow—and I'm certain at least three of the hits are intentional.

After about five minutes, they finally settle down. I lift my head again to check on them because they're *way* too quiet. They're just sitting there, glaring at one another.

"Um, guys?"

"I won."

"No, I won," Dallas argues.

I roll my eyes and sit up, bringing my knees up and curling my arms around them. "You both lost. So hush."

Maura mirrors my pose, sitting close enough to me that our elbows touch. She bumps me once and I can't help but smile. "Love you."

"You okay?" a gruff voice says. I can hear him holding back his emotions and I can't help but respect the guy for that. We just met a couple weeks ago, but I love that he's already attached enough to feel my hurt with me. To me, that means he's a keeper.

"Define 'okay.'"

Dallas throws an arm around me. "The exact opposite of not okay."

"Well, in that case, I'm pretty sure I'm not okay. I feel…"

"Empty," Maura says in a low, cracked voice. I look over at her and frown.

Dallas throws an arm around me, pulling me over to him and placing a gentle kiss on the side of my head. "You're not empty. That's the problem."

"Thank you for letting me stay here last night."

"You're welcome here anytime, Rae. You know that. But how about we don't *all* sleep in the same bed again? That was a little cramped. Because of Dallas's fantastic ass."

I laugh lightly and feel a tear slide down my cheek. I didn't even realize I was crying, and this surprises me a little. These are the first tears I've shed since Hudson told me about my dad. I didn't cry last night. I didn't cry when he told me. But right now, sitting here with my friends, I start crying. And it's an ugly one. I let it all out as Dallas scoops me into his arms and Maura rubs circles on my back.

"Maura, can you—"

"Already called him. He's on his way."

I nod, snuggling closer into Dallas's warmth.

"Dallas, have you lied to me since I've known you?"

"Of course not," he says. "If you've asked me something, I've always been truthful with my answers." I don't miss the way he phrases that, but I appreciate his clarification on it.

"Can we date instead?"

"Do you have a dick I don't know about?"

Laughing, I swat his chest. "No, you asshole."

"Then sorry, babe, but it's a no."

We're quiet a moment, sitting together, taking everything in. I haven't known Dallas all that long, and neither has Maura, but I feel like he's always belonged with us. He fits in perfectly and I'm really hoping he sticks around for a long damn time.

"Who did you call, Maura?"

"Perry. Remember the guy you met a couple weeks ago at the bar? The *really* drunk one you helped get outside? That's Rae's cousin."

Dallas stiffens for just a moment. *That's odd. Maybe they didn't have such a good encounter.* I pull out of his embrace and look him in the eyes. He's already learned of my obsession with eye contact. "Was he mean to you, Dall? He can be a dick when he's drunk."

The look in his eyes is haunted, remorseful, even. "N-no. He just reminded me of a ghost from my past."

"Is that ghost the reason you're single?" Maura asks bravely. I love that she's been coming out of her shell like that since everything happened with Tucker. Even though they aren't together right now and she's still broken up about it, I can still see all the silent confidence he's given her in the last few months.

"Yes," Dallas admits. Then he pastes a fake smile on his lips. "But no man can keep me down for long. I'll get back in the groove one of these days."

I don't call him out on the fakeness, because right now, we're all faking it. And we all know it.

"Come in!" Maura shouts.

"Oh wow. That's real safe, Maura. What if it's a serial killer? Or what if we were all naked?"

Maura shoots him a look. "Why? Why did I invite you to live with me?"

"I'm telling you: it's the ass."

"Is there room enough for me in there with this dude's ego?"

I smile at the sound of Perry's voice. "I think we can squeeze you in."

He saunters into the room, looking sleepy but still adorable in his own special way. I can tell he had one of his "late nights" again. Before I can start in on him, he sends a small smile my way. "You good?"

I shake my head. "No, not really. But I will be."

Dallas stands up as Perry walks closer to the bed. He doesn't introduce himself, just throws a glance at Dallas. Narrowing my eyes at my cousin, I do the introductions for them. "Sorry, Dallas. Ignore my cousin's lack of manners. Perry, this is Dallas. Say hi."

Perry grunts in reply, ignoring Maura's new roommate entirely.

Dallas arches a brow and his response is cold. "Yeah, we've met. I'm gonna grab a shower, ladies. Holler if you need anything."

I glance over at Maura as he exits the room in a hurry. She just shrugs, letting me know she noticed the odd exchange as well.

Perry slides into where Dallas was just sitting and puts his arms around me for a hug. "I'm here, you know. Always."

I return his hug. "I know, Per, I know."

"But I'm pissed at Hudson. I thought he was one of the good guys."

"He is. That's the problem."

He sighs and squeezes me tighter for just a moment before letting me go. "So, what's the game plan? Ignore him? Talk to him?"

"Well, I have to talk to him. He's my boyfriend."

"That's not who I was talking about, Rae."

I dart my eyes away from his. "Right." I frown. "No. We're not going there. Not now."

Perry's sigh is a bit more agitated this time. "It's been close to a year, Rae. You need to talk to him sometime."

"I will, Perry. It's just…"

"No more excuses. It's time."

"Let it go for now, Per," Maura chimes in. "She needs a few days to clear her head. Okay? Just let it go for now."

He gives me an aggravated half-smile and zips his fingers across his lips.

"Thank you," I mutter.

"Told you, anything for you."

"Anything? Like…a pizza?" Maura asks. "I'm starving."

Pizza makes me think of Gaige. Gaige makes me think of Hudson. And Hudson makes me think of this hole that's gaping and aching in my chest right now. This hole that's eating me alive from the inside out, gnawing at me, begging me to pay attention to it. But I don't want to. Not yet. Maybe not ever.

Lie.

"It's like eight in the morning. You don't need a pizza."

"Maybe not, but I *want* a pizza," she pouts. "I thought you'd do anything for her, Perry. *Anything.* Lies!"

Perry gives her an incredulous look. "You're off your fucking rocker, you know that? Just plain insane."

"Insanely hungry."

At that, I laugh. And it almost feels good. *Almost.* But I keep laughing because right now I need to pretend to be okay or I'm going to end up in tears.

Maybe that's what I need though. Maybe I need to release all this pent up frustration and anger once and for all. Because I am that—angry. At my dad, Hudson, *myself.* I'm angry because my dad screwed me up, Hudson screwed me over, and *I* let them. But my anger does me no good. The only thing it morphs into is sadness. I don't *need* sadness right now. Right now I need relief. And I'm not going to find that by covering my tears in fake, forced laughs.

Before I know it, I'm crying again. And I hate it. But I also know that I *need* to cry. I have to get this out or it's going to eat away at me. I'm tired of letting shit pick and tear at me, pulling me apart, leaving scraps of myself behind. I. Am. Done.

"I'm not even going to ask something as stupid as, 'Are you okay,' because I know you're far from it right now," Perry says sternly. I think back to when Dallas asked those three words just thirty minutes ago and momentarily wonder what my cousin would say about that.

"I just want…him. But I'm *so* damn angry right now that I can't see straight. That's not going to make anything better. So, as much as not being around him is going to kill me, I'm going to take a few days and just…be."

Perry nods. "I think that's a good idea. And while you're at it, maybe think about talking to your dad?"

I sigh heavily. "I…okay. I'll think about it."

"If you're staying again, I call big spoon!" Dallas calls from the bathroom.

Perry scowls and I throw him an unsure glance. "What's your deal with him?"

"I just don't like him, okay? Drop it."

Dallas strolls into the bedroom with just a towel around his waist, his hard abs on display. I may be devoted to Hudson, and Dallas may bat for the same team as I do, but I can't help but admire him. He has to work hard for all that beauty that's on display.

From beside me I hear Perry's breathing pick up. Watching him, I notice his eyes grow darker and his eyebrows squeeze together tighter.

Dallas flexes his pecs and throws a cocky grin toward my cousin. "You like?"

Perry huffs and jerks his gaze away from the body on full display. He turns to me with an irritated spark in his eye and I just know he's going straight to the nearest open bar after this. "I…I've got shit to do," he tells me. "If you need me, call me."

I nod and hug him one last time, knowing full well that the next time I talk to him, he's going to be face down in a bottle of Jack. Like always.

As soon as we hear the front door close, Dallas lets out a

humorless laugh. "Your cousin is a real peach, Rae."

Shrugging, I say, "I have no idea what his problem is, but I swear he's not usually like this."

Dallas, who doesn't look too convinced, just nods and struts back out of the bedroom calling "Big spoon!" over his shoulder on the way out.

Maura laughs from beside me. "Men. Can't live with them, can't live without them."

I lie back on the bed, resting my hands on my flat stomach, crossing my ankles, and staring up at the ceiling. "Don't we both know it."

She mirrors my pose but reaches over to grab my hand. And that's the way we stay—relaxed on the bed holding hands. Holding on to each other, and most importantly, our hearts.

Chapter Eight

HUDSON

I hate this. All of this. It's been four days since I've seen or heard from Rae, and I've been pissed off every single one of them. Maura, who calls me every day, is the only reason I know she's doing okay. I wish like hell I could just talk with her, make her see my side of things. But she refuses to answer her phone or texts. Every day she ignores me is another day a small hole forms in my heart.

Which is exactly why I'm taking Joey to my mom's for a couple days. I'm miserable, and my heartbroken mood is rubbing off on my kid. She's asked me about ten times now where Rae is. It hurts so hard when I have to tell her she's gone to stay with friends for a few days. Every day when I answer her, Joey's little shoulders sink lower and lower. I know she's bound to break down at some point. Since I know *I'm* liable to do so too, I have no idea how to stop it.

"You ready to go, kiddo?" I call up the stairs to my daughter.

I hear her shuffle across the hall, her head popping around the corner at the top of the stairs. Her eyes are bloodshot and puffy—a sure sign she's been crying. *Fuck. Guess I'm too late in the whole breaking down thing.*

"I'm…I'm not going until Rae comes home," she sniffles.

Sighing, I walk halfway up the stairs, hoping to coax her down. "Joey, baby, we've talked about it. Rae is just staying with Maura for a couple days. Girl time. You get that, right?"

Her face crumbles and she begins to sob. My feet fly up the stairs on autopilot and I wrap my arms around her.

"Shh…shh. What's wrong? Why are you crying? She's coming back."

I want to take the words back as soon as they leave my mouth. Because what if she doesn't come back? Then what? Then not only have I lost the woman I'm madly in love with, but Joey's also lost the only person she's ever seen as a mother. I have to fight back my own tears at the thought.

"She…she won't," her voice trembles. "She's not coming back."

I pull back and cradle her face in my hands, wiping away her tears. "Why would you say that?" My voice is a little stern, but I *have* to know if there's something she knows that I don't.

"Because I made her leave."

I tip my head and wrinkle my brows in confusion. "What makes you think so?"

"I…I…" She struggles to get the words out, hesitant like she's scared she's going to get in trouble for saying anything.

"Joey, I need you to tell me why you think you made Rae leave. *Please.*"

"I…asked to go swimming again." She starts shaking, her little body wracked with sobs. "I'm sorry! I…I didn't mean to. She got real scared when I asked and I knew I was in trouble. I know you don't want me swimming with Rae, daddy. I'm sorry."

I squeeze my eyes shut and turn my head into my shoulder, breathing deeply so I don't completely lose it at just the thought of what happened almost one year ago. When I feel like I have myself composed, I turn back to Joey.

"First, you can swim with Rae. That's perfectly okay. What happened last year wasn't your fault or hers. Okay?" She nods. "Second, *you* did not, and will not, ever make Rae leave. Do you understand that, Joey?"

"But…I… She…"

"No, okay? No. Rae loves you *so* much. She will never, *ever* walk away from you." I look into her eyes, imploring her to listen to me, to hear me, to understand me. "I promise, bug. I *promise*."

When she shakily bobs her head up and down, sniffling away the rest of her tears, I know I've finally gotten through to her.

I gather her in my arms, holding her tight, hoping to squeeze away all of her worries. She hugs me back just as fiercely and, just for a moment, I let my own tears flow freely.

I did this. *I* made Joey feel like she's the one to blame for Rae not being here. Not only did I screw up my relationship with Rae, hurting her beyond belief, but I've also managed to make my kid cry in the process. *You've really fucked this one up, Hudson. Fix this. Now.*

Pulling away from Joey and smoothing her hair down, I give her a small smile. She returns it. I tap the end of her nose and she swats at my hand.

"There's my smiling girl."

Expectedly, she scowls. I laugh at how much she acted like Rae just then. My joy is only momentary as I realize I just laughed for the first time since Rae left. I don't like that. I don't like laughing. It makes me feel like I've forgotten about what I've done. And I don't want to forget.

I stand, looking down at Joey, whose shoulders are no longer sagging. "Now, are you ready to go? Did you pack a bag? Nanna has clothes and stuff for you still, but I know she doesn't have your favorite pillow or pjs."

Joey darts down the hall and I make my way down the stairs. She returns just seconds later with a Finn *Adventure Time* backpack slung over her shoulder, carefully making her way down the stairs.

"I'm ready," she announces as she stands in front of me.

I quirk up my eyebrow at her, placing a lazy grin on my lips. "Last one to the car is the loser?"

She rolls her eyes and sighs. "You're already a loser."

Then she's gone, scurrying out the door in an instant, beating me to the car before I even get the front door closed.

She's already buckled into the back when I get in the car, bouncing in her seat, her gloomy attitude changed dramatically. Smiling at her in the rearview mirror, I twist around, placing my arm on the passenger seat and watching the road as I carefully maneuver out of the driveway. When I get onto the road, I start to turn back around, pausing only when a small hand lands on my arm.

"Dad?" I look back at my perfect, dark-haired angel. "She's gonna come home, right?"

My eyes start to sting and my throat gets tight. Swallowing thickly, I nod stiffly. "Of course, bug. She'll come back."

I hope.

"I'm so sorry, Hudson. Just…I'm sorry. I didn't want this to blow up in your face. I mean, I kind of expected it, but I was hoping my daughter would react differently."

I clench my jaw, wishing for just a split second that I could grab Ted by the shoulders and shake him. I want to yell and scream that this was all his fault. But that wouldn't be fair. This is just as much my fault as it is his. I've been wrong from the start to go behind Rae's back. I should have been honest and up front from the very beginning. But I wasn't. And neither was Ted. Now we're both paying for it.

I give him a strained smile. "It's okay, man. She'll, uh, come around."

"Damn, son. You don't sound even a little bit convinced, you know?" When I don't give any response to that, Ted squints at me, studying me closely. "Did you ask her? Did you propose a future with my daughter while still hiding this from her?"

My throat feels all scratchy, like I've been stuck out in the desert with no water for days. I take a sip from the glass I've been rolling between my hands. "Uh, kind of." Ted arches a challenging brow. "Fine. I did," I huff.

He lets out a big whoop, throwing his head back and slapping his knee, laughing his ass off at me.

"Goddamn, kid. You're… That's… Damn. You're brave." He shakes his head and I duck mine, not understanding how he thinks this is the funniest thing he's heard all day.

"And stupid beyond all belief." I swing my head back toward him, scowling within a nanosecond. "What? You know it as well as I do. That was a dumb move, Hudson. Really damn dumb. She's not going to trust another proposal you make for a long time."

I snort, taking another sip off my drink. "She'd have to come home first."

His eyebrows shoot up at this new bit of information. "She's gone?"

I nod. "Yep. Staying with Maura for a bit."

Ted frowns, scrubbing his hand over his head. "You've talked with her?"

"Nope. She won't answer my calls or texts. And trust me, I've left a lot. She's probably got a damn restraining order on my ass already."

His laugh is dry. "I doubt that, son. I've seen the way she looks at you. She's mad, but she's not *that* mad."

"Do you think she'll come back?" The words leave my mouth before I can catch them and stuff them back in.

"There's no way she won't, Hudson. Rae's a fighter, but more than that, she's a lover. She loves your daughter. She won't leave her. And she won't leave you. I know it seems like the end of everything right now, but I can feel it in my heart that it's not. Can't you?"

I reflexively clutch my chest, thinking about Rae and what it would feel like to lose her now. I sense this…spark. Something ignites in me and it's fierce. It's telling me to fight, to push, that it's not the end for us. I can *feel* it. And it gives me this new sense of hope that was slowly fading away.

Ted smiles, knowing exactly what's happening. "Good, son. That's good. Use that." He pauses briefly, scooting forward to the edge of the kitchen chair and folding his hands under his chin. Sadness washes over his face before he smiles again. "Erin and I, we had our troubles. Some of them fairly similar to what's going on with you and Rae right now. Now, I'm not saying fixing this is going to be easy. I'm not saying it'll happen overnight. But I *am* saying it will happen. I know my daughter, Hudson. *You* know my daughter. She won't walk away that easily. And I know you won't either. That fight you two have? That's all you need. The rest will fall into place."

God do I hope that's true.

He slaps his hand on the table. "Know what you need? A beer. And so do I. What do you say? Beer and wings at Clyde's?"

A fleeting, sinking feeling in my stomach tells me that's a bad idea, but I'm so eager to just get out of my own head right now, I ignore it. "Yeah, that sounds great, actually."

So that's what we do. I follow Ted in my car over to Clyde's, the same bar where Rae used to work that holds many memories of the two of us. The first thing I do as we pull in is scope out the lot for Maura's car. I let out a relieved breath when I don't see it and head inside behind my hopefully soon-to-be father-in-law.

We find a table and I do everything I can to suppress a groan when my least favorite waitress, Clarissa, sashays up to our table. So not the person I want to deal with right now. Not after she tried hitting on me in front of Rae—twice—in the last six months. I don't have the energy to deal with that shit today, and I'm liable to snap at any moment.

To my surprise, she's very cold and methodical as she asks for our drink order and hurries off. Silently saying a thank-you to whoever's looking out for me today, I glance down at the menu and spot what I want within seconds.

"What. The. Hell."

My spine goes straight and I seek out the person the shrill voice belongs to. I find her in a flash, rooted in the front of the hallway that leads out back to the employee hangout with Maura standing next to her. Apparently whoever *was* looking out for me just decided to go on break for the day. *Thanks, Guardian Asshole.*

In the four days I haven't seen her, I swear she's lost at least five pounds that she didn't have to lose in first place. I hate the way her eyes look swollen and her lips look chapped, like she just got done crying, and how the spark that's usually lighting them into a bright forest green has gone out. She looks as miserable as I feel, which is pretty damn miserable.

I'm ashamed to admit I'm momentarily thrilled that she's taking this as hard as I am, but then I check myself. She's probably a lot more upset over the reasons we're apart rather than us actually *being* apart.

And fuck if that doesn't claw at me.

The first thing that registers across her face is hurt. The second is sadness. But it's the third that has me ducking my head.

Rae is fucking pissed. Angry. *Fuming.*

Over the raucous customers and steady music, I hear her stomp across the bar, halting when she's about five feet from our table. I peek over at her to find her mouth twisted into an angry flat line, her nostrils flaring just a smidge. I so badly want to reach out and calm her, but I know right now my touch would have the opposite effect.

"Rae, it's not his…"

She holds her hand up, silencing her father. Her eyes never leave mine, heat blazing behind her stare. I see her work her jaw back and forth, fighting the words that want to spew out. Taking a calming breath, she lowers her hand and takes a step closer to me, and the heat turns into a low simmer, eventually being replaced by pools of tears that are threatening to spill over the ledge.

I can't breathe. I mean, I *can*, but I'm *scared* to. I want to pretend I'm seven years old again and my imaginary friend is helping me play invisible to my aggravated parents. I want to act like I'm not here, like I'm not breaking the heart of the woman I love.

"I…I can't right now, Hudson. *This?* With him? Four days later and *this* is what you're doing? Just hanging out like old friends, acting like nothing is wrong in your world?"

I want to reach out, to shake her, make her realize I am completely fucking broken right now. That these last four days have been nothing short of hell for me. That I sent my kid away for a few days because I couldn't handle just waking up and getting out of the damn bed. But I don't. Because I *deserve* this, this hurt. It's owed to me.

She stands there, waiting for me to say something, to defend my actions, maybe even lie again. I won't. So instead, I say something honest, something I think we both need to hear and be reminded of.

"I love you."

The fucking pool overflows and a tear slides down her cheek. I reach out, barely grazing her face. She flinches, moving away from my touch. And not just moving away by a few inches, but she turns around and bolts out the door. With my fucking heart in the palm of her hands.

I push my stool back to run after her, ignoring the hard stares I'm getting from everyone in the bar as it scrapes angrily across the floor. Ted calls after me, but I don't fucking care.

Slamming open the front doors, not even stopping when it slaps against the building, I run toward my girl, grabbing her arm and spinning her around to face me.

She gasps, peering up at me with sad, broken eyes. I crush my lips to hers before I can even think about it, pulling her into my embrace and cradling her head in my hands. She falls into me instantly, her body lining up with mine. Her hands clutching my chest, holding fistfuls of my shirt, dragging me in closer. If mouths could do so, ours would be making magic in this moment. We pour everything into this kiss. Our frustrations, pent up tension, broken hearts, tears…love. Lots and lots of fucking love. I feel the tiniest of pinpricks start in my chest, the little gaping holes sewing themselves shut every time our tongues tangle together. Magic. Pure fucking magic.

But just as quickly as the magic began, it ends. Suddenly, she's not begging me closer, but pushing me away. She's not holding on to me with everything she has, not wanting to let me go, but instead pleading for distance.

I pull back, still holding on to her, and tilt her head to mine, meeting her lust- and anger-filled gaze. We're taking staggered breaths, chests bumping against one another with every drag of air.

She opens her mouth to say something, closes it, and then opens it again. I don't let her. Instead, I kiss away her words. And she lets me.

She fucking lets me.

This kiss is less desperate, slower. And sadder. We both feel it, both feel the tears slide down her cheeks. And we ignore it because this kiss is just that perfectly tragic. So tragic that this sort of feels like…the end. *I don't want this to be the end.*

I'm the one to pull away first. Closing my eyes and dropping my forehead to hers, I speak. "I'm not going to let you stop loving me."

"Never."

That's all I need. That promise that no matter what, she'll love me. With that one little word, I feel stronger, safer, more sure. *We can do this.*

Taking an encouraging breath, I step away from her fully, putting at least a foot of distance between us. A little crinkle forms between her brows, her sudden irritation a little confusing. Especially when she was the one who just walked out—again—and the one who was just pushing me away moments ago.

"Take it, Rae. The time that you need, take it. I don't care how long it is—take it. We're going to make it through this because I'll never stop loving you, and damn if I don't know that our love *is* enough. I won't give up that easily and I don't think you will either. So take your time. I'll be here waiting for you when you're ready."

Spinning on my heel, I start marching back toward the bar, only to pause when I hear her feet on the pavement behind me. I twist around just as she reaches out for me, grabbing her hand and pulling her in for a hug. We stand in the parking lot holding on to each other for hours. Or maybe just minutes. Either way, it's too short of a time.

"Thank you," she says, her husky voice muffled by my chest.

Kissing the top of her head, I gently unwind my arms, stepping away once again.

Away from her. Away from my forever.

For now.

Chapter Nine

RAE

"As much as I hate saying this…you need to get the hell off my couch, woman. Now."

I glare at my blonde bestie, who's currently standing between me and my boys on the flat screen.

"The Winchesters are on."

"Who cares about the friggin' Winchesters!"

I gasp at her words because *everyone* cares about the Winchesters. Or at least they should.

"You stink, Rae. I mean you're downright rank smelling. Get. Up. Shower. Get dressed. Go pick up pizza instead of ordering delivery. I don't care, just get the hell off my couch!"

I sigh and grumble all at once, waving her out of the way. She doesn't budge.

"Ugh! Fine!" I yell, throwing the blanket off me and jumping up from the couch. "But I'm *not* shaving my legs!"

"Fine! They keep me warm at night anyway!"

Fifteen minutes later I waltz back out the bathroom feeling—and

I'd hate to admit this to Maura—refreshed and a lot more like myself than the zombie I've become.

I catch Maura snuggled up on the couch under *my* blanket, watching *my* show. I clear my throat, standing in front of the TV just like she did when she interrupted my pity party.

"What?" she asks, innocently blinking up at me. "It's a good show, okay? And besides, you're kicked out of the apartment for the day. It's my turn to wallow."

Sometimes I forget I'm not the only one hurting right now, that I'm not the only one going through a…separation. I feel a little guilty for making this all about me the past four days, since I accidentally encountered Hudson at Clyde's when I was visiting with Maura on her last day there. And then proceeded to make out with him in the parking lot, only to have him push me away and say beautiful words that simultaneously ripped my heart to shreds and stitched it up. I almost forgot I was mad at him for just the tiniest of moments.

Then reality set in, and she's a real bitch. My anger came back quick. But somehow, it was lessened. And I was genuinely confused about how to feel regarding that. Because I *want* to be mad. I just don't know if I *need* to be mad.

My cell buzzes on the glass coffee table, making me jump a little. Maura must sense my hesitation to grab it because she says, "It's just Elle. She's texted twice now."

Elle: Joey's been asking for you…

Then…

Elle: Think you can come by today? I promise not to do some weird thing like trap you and Hudson together to make you talk.

I laugh because that's *so* something she'd do.

I quickly type back a "yes" and announce to Maura I'm heading out.

"Ohmygod. It's about time! Your sadness was sucking up all the air."

Ignoring her, I head to the front door and blow her a kiss. "Love you, Maurie."

"So inconsiderate," I hear her grumble as I pull the door shut behind me.

I run smack into a hard chest, stumbling backward.

"Shit. Sorry, Rae," Dallas says, reaching out and steadying me.

"Good God you're like a damn brick! You sure you don't like girls? Because *shit*."

"I'm about as sure of that as you are about loving Hudson." He winks.

I roll my eyes at his new cheesy attempt to get me to talk to my maybe boyfriend. He's been doing it for days now. Sometimes it's cute and funny, other times it's irritating beyond belief. I do love how he's making an effort, though. Dallas has become a good friend since he moved here.

"Finally leaving the house, huh? Good. You were starting to smell."

"I was not! You have no damn manners, Dallas Middle Name Montgomery."

"Golly. Can't believe you got my middle name right!" he teases on a fake southern drawl. He scratches his nose uneasily at my confused smirk. "Sorry, I tend to pretend I'm from the South sometimes. I've always secretly wanted to be a Texan. Ya know, so I could have a cool accent."

"Where are you from, anyway?"

He shrugs noncommittally. "Around."

I let his non-answer slide and we trade places. "I'm heading to

Elle's, so…" I lift my chin toward the door. "Keep an eye on her, will ya? Think she's having a bad day."

"Which one?"

I frown, knowing he's asking which Bentley brother she's upset over—Tanner or Tucker. "Both, I think."

He nods. "Knew she was bound to have a shit day soon. She's been a little too…peppy. And you know as well as I do what happens when she's like that."

"The crash."

"Yep."

"And my being here and moping about isn't helping her heal at all."

Dallas reaches out and grabs my hand, giving it a tight squeeze. "No, don't say that. It's not you, sweetheart. It's just…well, life. We all have our demons. We'll fight 'em off together."

"Promise?"

He winks again. "Of course."

Dropping my hand, he turns to the apartment door, grasping the doorknob and giving it a slight twist. I turn around and head down the walkway.

"Rae?"

I turn, glancing over my shoulder at him.

"You're gonna be okay."

My shoulders slump because I don't feel like those words will ever be true again.

"I know," I whisper.

He shakes his head. "No, not just you, but you and Hudson. You're both going to be okay. You're gonna make it out of this. If there's one couple I have faith in, it's you two. Felt it from the moment I met you both. You're his forever."

I feel this sorely missed flutter in my chest at his words. Because that's something Hudson's said to me before. *His forever.* And I want to be that more than anything.

"Rae!"

Joey launches herself at me, wrapping her small arms around my middle instantly. I return the hug with equal ferocity. I've missed this kid so much. I want to kick myself right in the ass for walking away from her while Hudson and I try to work this out, but I need my space. Just sucks that space away from him had to mean space away from the little girl who's felt like a daughter to me for the last year.

Pulling her away, I hold her at arm's length, glancing her over. I swear she's grown at least two inches since that last time I saw her eight days ago.

Eight days? Has it already been that long? Fuck.

"How you doin', kiddo?"

"Good. Dad says he misses you."

I blink back the instant tears and nod. "I know, bug. I miss him too."

"When are you coming home?"

I open my mouth and close it again, struggling to find an appropriate answer.

"Joey Tamell! What did I tell you about asking her that? That's impolite," Elle scolds as she comes around the corner, stepping into the small entryway. She smiles at me, her eyes glassy with unshed tears. "Rae." She enfolds me in the warmest hug I've had in days. "I've missed you, girl."

"I've missed you too, Elle."

She wipes at her eyes when she pulls away. "Sorry, sorry. I promised myself I wouldn't cry when I saw you, but I can't help it."

"Trust me, I've been telling myself that same thing all morning."

She laughs lightly. "Well, come on in, dear. I've made us some sandwiches. We can eat lunch with Joey and then maybe talk."

Elle doesn't give me the chance to respond that I'm not hungry. Instead, she ushers me into the kitchen, Joe hot on our heels.

"Turkey's fine, right?"

"Yes, thank you. You didn't have to make lunch. I haven't had much of an appetite lately, but this thing looks damn good."

"A quarter!" Joey says, sticking her hand out for my swear jar payment.

"Just a quarter? I thought it was seventy-five cents now."

She wrinkles her pert little nose at me. "You want to pay more?"

Laughing, I shake my head. "No way. But I don't feel right getting special treatment either."

She shrugs. "Dad says you're sad. I don't like that, so I thought I'd cut you a deal."

The smile falls off my face rather quickly. *Has Hudson been talking about me? How much does Joey know about what's been going on?*

"Ya know, how about you go ahead and take your sandwich into the living room, Bug. You can watch some *Adventure Time* while you eat," Elle offers, sensing my unease.

"Okay!" Joey grabs her plate and cup of juice, scurrying out of the kitchen in a flash.

I take a bite of my lunch, ignoring the stare I feel from Elle.

"She doesn't understand what's going on. And Hudson hasn't said anything to her. In fact, she's been staying over here for the last few days. A mini-vacation, if you will."

I peel my eyes from the worn out spot on the kitchen table I was gazing at, meeting her clear blue eyes.

"I was worried he'd brought her into this."

She frowns. "He'd never do that, Rae. You know him better than that."

"I thought I knew him, Elle. I don't feel like I do anymore." The last part comes out a choked whisper, and she reaches her hand over to soothe me. "Almost a year. That's how long he's been lying to me. Almost our entire relationship. How do I trust that?"

Her eyes grow soft and sympathetic. "I can be frank with you, yes?" I nod immediately. "You're like a daughter to me, Rae, so I say this with love… So what?"

My mouth drops open. *So what? He lied! That's what!* I'm getting ready to say just that when she holds her hand up.

"Hear me out, okay? I know my son. *You* know my son. He wouldn't have had secret meetings with your father if he didn't have a damn good reason to do so. That's not him. Think about it from his side, Rae. He's a father. Do you think he'd want Joey to cut off contact with him for trying to protect her? Not that I'm saying what Ted did was okay, because honestly, I'm a little pissed off at him myself for it, but I don't think you're seeing this from their perspective at all."

I chew on my lip, trying to do just that. My father didn't directly lie about what happened with my mother. I've always known she committed suicide. The only thing he did was not confirm whether or not my drowning night after night was a nightmare or a memory. I also never asked. Hell, he put me in therapy to help cope with it, but even my own mind blocked me from the pain. That had to mean something.

In all honesty, I know I'd have eventually forgiven my father for not being straightforward with me. Because I *can* see his side of things. I just still needed some time, needed space to figure out how I'd apologize for blocking him out of my life after he'd done so much to protect me. And to figure out how I was going to let him back in. I just needed time. It hurts that Hudson didn't let me have it.

But…that's something else entirely. Hudson and his lies. I can't justify those. He should have been honest with me, especially after what I'd just discovered about my father and his inability to fully tell the truth. But he wasn't. He snuck around and hid things from me. He formed a friendship with my father, something I didn't have anymore. That hurt too.

Admittedly, I can see where Hudson's coming from as well. His desire to keep some sort of thread between my father and me is somewhat admirable. I know I was stretching and dragging that tiny piece of thread out dramatically, and I'm sure my father wasn't innocent in begging for information either. That had to be slowly eating at him. The problem here is his lack of honesty. I thought we were better than keeping shit from each other, especially heavy issues like that. And now I'm questioning everything. It makes me feel sick that he could so easily hide something so big from me.

I clutch my stomach like I could physically get ill at any moment.

"It's not all black and white, huh?"

Elle's voice drags my eyes upward. "It never was. That's the problem."

"I don't envy you, Rae. I don't blame you for being upset. Hell, *I'm* upset. But I'm also a little disappointed that you're fighting trying to understand so hard. Hudson doesn't deserve that. Joey doesn't deserve that. And neither do you."

"I also don't deserve lies."

She sighs. "No, but you do deserve a man that's willing to protect you and take care of you at all costs, no matter the risks. You have that."

I did.

"Don't do that. Don't think in past tense."

"How did you..."

Her shoulders lift slightly. "It's a mom thing."

I laugh and it seems to shake the heavy fog of sadness that's hanging around. The room feels lighter and so do I. A little.

"Thank you, Elle. I... Just thank you."

She smiles warmly at me. "All I want is for you to be happy, Rae. I've grown fond of you over this past year. Your happiness means something to me now." A hint of sadness creeps into her eyes. "And even if that means not being with my son anymore, that's okay. No matter what you decide, I'll always be here for you."

Startling both of us, I jump out of my chair and throw my arms around her neck, hugging her close and tight.

"I wish some days you were my mom," I quietly admit, pulling away from her.

She laughs and pats my cheek. "That would be very awkward, darling. I'm secretly hoping you're going to stay with my son and that's just not something I can condone."

I stayed at Elle's for a couple hours, laughing and catching up with Joey. We played two board games and watched a few cartoons. Having her around helped heal me a little. It felt natural, normal. I missed it. I missed the role of parent, our story times and movie parties. Our...

Who am I kidding? I miss Hudson. I miss Joey. I miss my fucking family.

Plopping down on a rock sitting just on the edge of Lake Quannapowitt, I pull my phone from my pocket. Flipping it between my hands, I contemplate calling Hudson. I want to talk to him, to hear his voice, to tell him I still love him. But I'm scared to because I am still upset. Even though Elle gave me some more insight into things today, I'm still holding on to some anger. Or something that closely resembles it.

I still feel…off.

Rather than calling him, I decide on sending a text. I flip my phone over just in time to hear a masculine and sexy voice say, "Hello?"

I freeze. It's the exact voice I've been wanting to hear, and it sends chills down my spine. Just that one single word conjures up all my repressed desires. I can feel my nipples harden into little pebbles and that old familiar stirring happens. God I fucking miss him. His smile, his laughter, his voice, his touch—all of it.

"Hello? Rae?"

I pull myself out of the daze I'm in, lifting the phone to my ear. I can hear him breathing on the other end.

"Rae? Are you there?"

I don't answer. I'm not ready to.

"Shit." He sighs. "I know you're there. I…fuck." I can picture him sitting behind his office desk, lowering his head, his biceps bulging as he nervously squeezes the back of his neck. "I'm sorry, Rae," he whispers hoarsely. "*So* fucking sorry. I love you. I miss you. God I fucking miss you."

I smile at his use of the same words I was just thinking. I like that our connection is so strong even when we're so far apart.

"Rae, you have to know that I only went to see him at first because I knew you wouldn't but wanted to."

At first? What the hell does that mean?

"I did it for you. I didn't mean to lie about it for so long. It just grew into something that I knew you wouldn't understand at the time. So I didn't tell you. But…I regret that now. And I'm…I'm sorry.

Fuck!"

He shouts the curse word, the voice inside my head shouting it along with him. After talking with Elle today, I'm starting to understand his side of things more. I get why he hid it for so long. If he'd have come home after his first visit, so soon after everything happened, I'd have flipped out. We'd have fought like crazy and I'm not sure we'd have recovered at the time. I was in such a sensitive state emotionally that I don't think I would have reacted rationally. Not that what happened when he confessed was rational, but the amount of time that's passed with his lies justified that reaction. At least to me.

But now I need to know just exactly what's happened with my dad this past year. I need to know everything he's told him, to know how many of my secrets have been shared. And I need to know what drove him to keep hiding things from me.

"Can we talk?" he asks quietly. "And I don't just mean hang out in the silence like this but *really* talk? Please?"

I'm not ready for that.

"You're not ready for that, I get it." The way he knows me amazes me. "So we can text. Please. It's better than nothing at this point." I hear a faint knock on the other end, one of his employees probably. "Shit. I've got to go." A pause. "Just…text me. Okay? I want to hear from you." Another pause. "I love you. I miss you."

The line goes dead.

I slowly pull the phone away from my ear, staring down at the black screen. What do I do with that? With the turmoil I hear in his voice? He sounds as miserable as I do. He sounds…broken.

Before I can stop myself, I shoot off a text to him.

Me: What's your favorite animal?

Chapter Ten

HUDSON

The smile that crosses my face is instant. She's playing our game, Five. You can bet your sweet ass I'll play right back.

Me: An otter. What's your best kept secret?

I know I'm playing with fire sending that question, but it's the first thing I thought of.

Rae: I drink from the jug of orange juice all the time. And I yell at anyone else that does it because it's MY orange juice. What's yours?

Me: I ate the yellow snow one time.

Rae: OMG. How old were you?

Me: I was four. Or six. Same difference. (Counting this as a question.)

Rae: I never want to kiss you again.

That's a damn lie.

Me: What's a lie you just told?

Rae: I never want to kiss you again.

Me: What's your favorite quote? Mine is "Fuck bitches,

get money."

Rae: Liar. "Crap has always happened, crap is happening, and crap will continue to happen." What's really yours?

Me: Don't have one. Who said that?

Rae: I'm counting this as one of the five. Chuck Palahniuk.

Smartass.

Me: Was that you who called?

Two minutes—I count—go by before she answers.

Rae: Yes. Wouldn't it suck if it wasn't?

Me: I'm glad I didn't mention the time I ate the yellow snow when I was sixteen, then…

Rae: OMG. Are you joking?

Me: Sorry, out of questions.

Rae: HUDSON!

Me: RAE!

Me: I love you.

Rae: I know.

I stare at my phone for minutes, waiting for another reply, *needing* another reply.

I don't get one.

"Who the fuck just killed a kitten? You look depressed, man."

I didn't even notice Gaige walk into my office. Partially because the door was open from when Liam popped his head in a few minutes ago, and also because I was so consumed by my little text exchange with Rae. Or her lack of real response. Whatever.

"Hey, man."

He raises a brow at me, folding his arms over his chest. "What's going on?"

"I was just texting Rae."

"Like, as in she participated too?"

"Yep. Full blown conversation. We…we did Five." I can't stop the twitch to my lips just thinking of us going back to our roots, playing that silly five-question game in the beginning of our relationship.

Gaige's eyes go wide, catching the significance. "Five? But that's awesome! Why do you look sad?"

"I told her I loved her."

"Okay…"

"She said, 'I know.'"

His lips slam into a flat line in a nanosecond, his hands finding his hips. He stands there, looking deep in thought. Or constipated. I'm not sure which.

"Well, good."

I throw my arms up. "What the fuck do you mean 'good'? How is that *good?*"

He shrugs. "I don't see how it's bad."

"It's not even a real damn response!"

Again with the fucking shrug. "But it's *some* sort of response. Better than radio silence."

Throwing myself back in the chair dramatically, I sigh. "How the fuck do women even like you? You're like this giant bag of…dicks."

"Did you just call me a bag of dicks?"

"Don't be one."

"Because I said it's good she's even responding to you? Are you hearing yourself? Wait. Are you going crazy? You're not making any sense."

"You're not sense!"

Lifting his hands like he's Chris fucking Pratt warding off those ferocious little velociraptors, he says, "Right. Let's pretend you didn't just fly off the handle and move on, huh?"

I glare at him.

"Right," he repeats. "You want to go to Clyde's tonight? I know Joe's still at Elle's, so I'd figured I'd invite ya out. Just eat some grub, grab a few beers, maybe watch a game or some shit."

"No."

"Want to just get rip-roaring drunk?"

"Yes."

It feels like my head is Santa's workshop and a dozen or so little elves are making about a hundred toys per minute.

Getting drunk sucks.

Lie.

Getting drunk is fun. It's the hangover that sucks.

Gaige and I decided getting drunk was something that "needed" to happen. So we did. Or I did. He stayed sober. All I remember is going to Clyde's, eating a basket of fries, doing five shots of Patrón, guzzling down three beers, and then washing that all down with two shots of Jameson. And we were only there an hour. Yeah, I was begging for this fucking hangover.

Gaige drove me home—but not before I puked down the side of my car out the window—tucked me into bed, and left me to my own devices after he made sure I wasn't going to swallow my own barf in my sleep.

Such a good friend. (Note the sarcasm there.)

"Knock, knock!" Liam hollers, walking right in my office. "You look like shit, boss."

I groan, holding my head in my hands. His voice sounds like someone took a pillowcase full of silverware and shook it up real fast.

And I *hate* the sound of silverware clinking together.

"Heard you got pretty wasted last night."

Peeking up at him, I glare but don't answer.

"Heard you even puked down the side of your car."

My stomach twists into knots at the thought and I press my hand to it, trying to hold back the vomit climbing its way up my throat.

"Shit. Sorry. Anyway, your girl is here. Want me to send her back?"

I spring out of my chair in an instant, the nausea hitting me so hard I reach for the trash can and actually *do* vomit this time.

"Yeah, I'm out. I'll give ya five and send her back," he says, hightailing it out of the room.

I empty my stomach, which turns out to be mostly liquid, starting to feel a little more like myself with every heave. Straightening back up, I wipe my mouth and look around for the extra bottle of mouthwash I stashed in here years ago. I take a swig, cringing at the stale taste. Swish, spit, repeat. I do a breath check and decide I'm good to go.

Then I realize I'm not so good because I've been pacing for the past two minutes.

Rae's coming to see me. On her own. She's taking the initiative in this. She *wants* to see me. Does this mean she's ready to move forward? To forgive? Because I'm *so* fucking ready for that.

Wait…what if she's not? What if she's here to break this off officially? FuckfuckFUCK.

"H-Hudson?" My head snaps toward the door at the sound of her voice. I swear it, my fucking knees go weak and I have to grab hold of the corner of my desk to keep me stable. *Or maybe that was just the sudden movement and little bit of wooziness from the booze still hanging around. Yeah, that seems more logical.*

"Rae." I smile at her, motioning to the chairs on the visitor's side of the desk. "Come sit. I'm glad to see you."

She wrings her hands together, obviously nervous about something, and takes a seat next to me. Panic rolls over my spine. *Maybe she is here to make this break official.* I gulp loudly. I can't take it if that's what she's here to do.

Remember when you were younger and you played the Quiet Game with your friends? The one who stays quiet the longest gets the loser's chocolate milk at lunch? That game you always tried your hardest to win? It feels like we're both playing that now. To the extreme. That's how silent the room is right now—Quiet Game winner worthy, and it looks like neither one of us is ready to give up our chocolate milk.

I take a deep breath, deciding that's a risk I'm willing to take. She jumps a little at the sound, tilting her head to glance up at me.

"What—" I clear my throat, the nervousness creeping in, and try again. "What are you doing here, Rae?"

Confusion coats her face, and her eyes grow cautious and unsure.

"Oh, no. It's not that I'm not happy to see you—because I am—I'm just wondering why you're here," I reassure her, realizing my question sounded like I didn't want her here.

This doesn't do anything to clear her eyes of uncertainty.

I sit up in my chair, not sure why she's still looking at me like I've gone insane. "Um, did I say something wrong?"

"You invited me, Hudson. Last night."

I invited her? When…?

"Oh shit."

"What?"

"Huh?"

"You said, 'oh shit.' Why?"

I groan, grabbing my head and giving it a good squeeze, trying to get the stupid to fall out. *Must be stuck, dumbass.*

"Did I…call you last night?"

She shakes her head. "No, you texted."

I did? I pull my phone from my pocket, opening up my texts to see what all I sent in my drunken haze.

Me: Tpmrrw? Seee yu? Come bye?

Rae: Yes.

I want to laugh at my atrocious spelling skills, but I don't. All I can focus on is that Rae responded within seconds and ignored all the signs pointing to drunk. Because she wanted to see me too.

Pocketing my phone, I stare at her, her lips pursed, waiting for an answer of some sort. "I, uh, kinda got wasted last night. That was a desperate drunken text."

I feel the heat radiating off her. She's angry. I just don't know why. I'd be flattered as hell if I was the only thing someone could think about when they were drunk.

"You were out last night, partying it up, huh? During all of this shit we're going through, you decide it's a good idea to go out and get hammered? With who? Fuckin' chick magnet Gaige himself? Great, Hudson. That's just great."

I lift my hands up, holding them out to her, surrendering to this war I had no idea we were in. "Hold the phone. I went out to clear my head, to relax a little. That's all that was." That doesn't seem to ease her at all. "And don't you dare bring Gaige into this. He doesn't deserve that hint of distaste in your voice. He's never done anything for you to believe he's anything but a damn saint and you know it. In fact, neither have I. I've never lie—"

I stop, catching my biggest mistake.

She sits forward in her chair, her eyes falling into slits. "No, please continue, Hudson. Go ahead and tell me how you've 'never lied' to me. Go for it. Lie right to my face. Again. I dare you."

I don't say anything, the venom in her words eating a hole in my heart.

"Nothing to say, Hudson? Fuckin' typical," she spits, shaking her head in obvious disgust.

Grabbing her bag, she lifts from the chair, and I panic. *She's leaving.* I grab at her wrist, closing my fingers around her, stopping her in her tracks.

"Stop. *Please.*"

She does.

Even though she hasn't turned around to look at me, I hang my head, the shame of my lies weighing me down. "Rae. I'd never do anything like you're suggesting, and you know that. Don't turn this shit with your dad into something it's not. That's not us. We don't do that."

Nothing. I tug gently on her wrist and she finally looks back at me, piercing me with her sad green eyes.

"We don't do *this.* We don't pick stupid fights over insane things. And we definitely don't walk out just because we're upset. I let you do it before, and if my sleepless nights and cold sheets are any indication, that was the biggest mistake I've made. Just please. *Please.* Stay."

She pulls her wrist free, marching around me and sitting back in her chair. Taking a calming breath, I follow her, sitting on the edge of my seat next to her. I reach out and pull her hand into my lap. She won't look at me, so I reach over and pull her face toward mine.

"We're done walking out. If we have shit to work through, we're doing it then. I don't want a relationship like that. I've had one before and they're shit."

She casts her eyes down, a tear making its way down her cheek. "That, what I accused you of, that was wrong. I'm sorry. You didn't deserve that." She pauses, collecting herself. "That's not me, Hudson. I…fuck! I don't know what's wrong with me. I feel like I'm going nuts."

I don't disagree with her, because I feel like *I'm* going nuts too. This whole thing just reeks of fuckedupness. It's gotten messy and ugly, and I hate it. I want our clean, beautiful, *easy* relationship back.

"I only went out last night because I can't fucking bear the thought of going back to an empty house. Joey's still at my mom's. I don't know how to tell her, to talk to her about any of this."

"Tell her what?"

I swallow, scared to say the words. "That you moved out."

Rae laughs and it's so damn beautiful. "I didn't *move out*, Hudson. I'm just clearing my head too. That's the only way that made sense at the time."

"I…I miss you. And I know that's not fair to say, but it's the damn truth. I want you back in our house, in our bed, in my life every damn day. I just…want you."

"I want that too."

"Then—"

"No," she interrupts. "I'm just… I still need some time, Hudson. I know that's not what you want to hear, and honestly, it might not even be the right answer, but it's the truth. Just…not yet."

I nod, not in agreement but because I don't trust myself to speak, especially since all I want to do right now is beg. Beg her to come home, to forgive me, to let me love her for the rest of our days. But I don't. I keep my mouth shut.

"I should go. I've got some work to do and you're probably busy catching up on work."

She gets up to leave again and I feel the panic hit me once more. *I don't have any plans to see her again.* "Go on a date with me!"

The words tumble out of my mouth, my eyes wide and surprised. Her reaction mirrors my own.

"O-okay," she agrees.

"Okay?"

"Okay. I would really love that."

I take a few steps toward her, crowding her against the office door, smirking down at her. "I'd *really* love that too."

She tries to turn away from my words, hiding a smile that's formed on her lips at my mocking her. I grab her chin and pull her face back to mine. I hold her gaze and lower my mouth to hers, sealing our lips together in a hard kiss. I feel her body start to sway, her tongue darting out, begging me to tangle mine up with hers. I pull back and peer down at her, my lips tingling with the memory of hers. She's breathless and her eyes are glazed over in a dense sexual haze, and I fucking love it.

I give her another quick kiss, ending it before she can even react. "How's Friday?"

"Huh?"

Chuckling, I say, "How's Friday for our date?"

She clears her throat, letting out a small sexy laugh. "Good."

"Good or *really* good?"

"*Really* good."

I smile, leaning down to close my lips over hers again, letting this one linger. It's slow and loving. The perfect mix of *I want to rip your clothes off* and *make slow, sweet love to me.* I wrap my tongue around hers at the same time I do my arm, using both as anchors. I cup her face, getting just the angle I want, exploring her mouth even further. I know it's time to back off when she lets out a low moan.

It takes another five seconds before I force myself to back away. Resting my head against hers when I do, I suck in air, letting the magic we create together settle around us, letting her feel how amazing things are with us, how fucking *right* they are.

"I love you, Rae," I whisper, my lips brushing lightly over hers with every word.

"I know."

Chapter Eleven

THE GAME OF FIVE

Rae: I'm secretly attracted to Channing Tatum…'s ass. Celebrity crush?

Hudson: eAsy. Emma Stone. See what I did there? (And don't make fun of my awesome taste in movies.)

Rae: Easy A reference. Nice. (Counting as question.) If you had to pick…smell horse poop the rest of your life or eat your least favorite meal every day?

Hudson: Your strangeness is a concern. Meal. Do you like chili cheese hotdogs?

Rae: Stop being gross, Hudson. It's unattractive. What's your favorite pet name? Like, for another person.

Hudson: Does asshole count?

Rae: Yes, and so does that question.

Hudson: Dammit. What's one thing you wish for almost daily?

Rae: Perk to start delivering coffee and scones. Yours?

Hudson: You.

Hudson: Shit. Sorry. It…it just came out. I'm sorry.

Rae: I miss you too.

Hudson: Does Friday make you nervous too?

Rae: Beyond.

Rae: Wait. Too? Does that mean you're nervous?

Hudson: Beyond. And that's Five.

Hudson: Are you ready for tomorrow?

Rae: No. You?

Hudson: Yes. And no. Five?

Rae: You're already down to 3. Make them good.

Hudson: I CAN'T HANDLE THAT SORT OF PRESSURE!

Rae: Suck it up.

Hudson: If you could own one thing, anything in the entire world, what would it be?

Rae: Hmm… Google. Then I'd be rich as hell. And smart. Google people are smart, right? (doesn't count!)

Hudson: I think so.

Rae: Then Google. You?

Hudson: Your heart.

Rae: OMG. CHEESEBALL! That was so LAME!

Hudson: You're welcome.

Rae: Crap. I think it actually worked. I feel…a smile.

Hudson: Again, you're welcome.

Rae: Maura is looking at me like I'm nuts because I keep

doing this weird groan/laugh thing.

Hudson: I'll just go ahead and add that to the list of noises of yours I like.

Rae: Add it? What else is on that list?

Hudson: You know…me making you moan is at the top.

Rae: You do that?

Hudson: *glare emoji*

Rae: Don't flake on me now! Answer the question.

Rae: Hudson?

Hudson: No. I quit. You win. Today.

Hudson: You ready to fall back in love with me today?

Rae: Back? I never stopped, you ass-butt.

Hudson: Just testing you, Squirrel.

Hudson: Quick Five?

Rae: Ready.

Hudson: Red or white wine?

Rae: Not a big wine person. White, I guess. Blue or green?

Hudson: Green. Turkey or ham?

Rae: Turkey. Dresses or jeans?

Hudson: As sexy as dresses are, jeans. More versatile. Favorite scent?

Rae: Like…candles? Fragrance? General?

Hudson: Any.

Rae: Cottonwood. And you.

Hudson: Did you just try to sweet talk me?

Rae: Guilty. Did you like it?

Hudson: Oh yeah.

Hudson: This is five… Do you think I've still got a shot?

Rae: Oh yeah. Do you believe in forever?

Hudson: Only with you.

Rae: Did you just try to sweet talk me?

Hudson: ;-) Sorry, babe, game's over. I'll see you soon. I love you.

Rae: I know.

Chapter Twelve

RAE

"A date, huh?"

"Yes, and I'm freaking out!" I shout, grabbing clothes from my poorly packed suitcase and throwing them onto Maura's bed. I mindlessly rifle through the unkempt pile, not really looking at anything but trying to keep my hands busy.

"You do realize you've already been dating him for the last year, right?"

I glare at my best friend. "You're not helping, Maura."

I think a lot of my nerves have to do with the fact that I haven't seen Hudson since our little argument at his office. Four days ago. We've been texting, playing Five, but it's not the same. This is a whole new game we're getting ready to play.

"Fine." She rolls her eyes and picks up a green shirt I have out on the bed. "How about this?"

Smiling, I pull it from her hands, hugging it to me. It's the shirt I wore on my first date with Hudson. *Of course* she would pick this shirt. Because it fits. It's perfect. And it's a damn sign if I ever got one.

"Good choice."

"Here," she says, shoving a dark pair of jeans at me. "Wear these too. You're welcome."

I quickly make my way to her adjoining bathroom to change. I walk back out to find her quietly talking with Dallas.

"…gonna hate you. These things never end well," I catch Dallas saying.

"What never ends well?" I question.

Dall turns to me with a small smirk. "Roommate's night out. We're having one tonight. We plan to get drunk."

"Yikes. Have fun with that one."

"Hopefully Perry doesn't ruin this one again."

I frown. "He's getting bad, huh? I honestly can't remember the last time he spent an entire day sober. I just…I don't know how to help him. Especially when he doesn't want it."

"I'm at a complete loss myself. He's stopped frequenting Clyde's since I quit. He's now taken up residence at Mic's. Gary's already thrown him out twice."

"Fuck."

"I, uh, I could try to talk with him." I look to Dallas, noting the concern in his voice, wondering where it comes from. "I mean, it's worth a shot. Maybe he'd take better to some advice from an outsider rather than his best friends."

I want to believe that's what Dallas means, but I can see something in him, something that's motivating him to want to help Perry, who's been nothing but a total dick to him. I'm just not sure what it is. Maybe there's just a layer to Perry that he connects with, can relate to on a level Maura and I can't.

"Um, yeah, that would be great, Dallas. Hopefully someone can get through to him. Thanks."

"Don't thank me yet. He's fairly determined to hate me, so this could be quite the adventure."

"Well, you're willing to try. That's all that counts. Speaking of trying…" Maura turns to me. "How are those nerves? You feeling any better?"

"Was until you just reminded me about them. It. The date."

"Oh, she's nervous all right. She's speaking in tiny sentences." Dallas laughs.

I glare at him. "Don't you have to go play head shrink or something?"

"And feisty. She's getting all worked up now," Maura teases.

"You're both evil."

"Oh, hush. You love us and you know it. Now go finish getting ready. Hudson will be here soon and you haven't even touched your hair yet."

"I'm going, I'm going," I tell her, finding my way back to the bathroom.

As I start to get ready, I notice the shake to my hands, the flutters of nerves in my stomach, the slight buzzing in my head. I have no clue why I'm so nervous. Maura was right—I've already been dating Hudson for just about a year. We've gone on countless dates, lived together, romanced our way into love. This should be no different, especially considering all we've done together and been through. But it is. The way this feels? It's…new. This feels like a complete do-over.

And I'm so ready for that.

A knock sounds at the front door, startling me so hard I drop the can of hairspray I'm holding, letting it clatter loudly to the floor.

The sudden tapping on the bathroom door makes me yelp. "You okay in there, Rae?" Dallas asks, twisting at the knob and inching the door open.

I peer at him through the crack. "I…fuck."

He opens the door fully, refusing to let me use it as a barrier, a safe spot. Crowding into the small bathroom, he places his hands on my shoulders, steadying me.

"Chill. You're going to be fine. Just take deep breaths."

"I don't know why I'm so nervous," I admit, pulling away to glance in the mirror one last time. *Is he going to think this outfit is stupid? Is he even going to remember it?*

"Because you're madly in love with him and you realize that this is an opportunity to start over, to make things right, to make them better. Because you're smart. You'd be insane to not be nervous." He pauses for a second. "Rae, Hudson's a good guy. I don't know him all that well, but I can tell you that he doesn't want to hurt you. Just…give him a chance, okay?"

I nod, thinking back to my earlier text exchange with Hudson. "I plan to."

"Good. Now go out there and get that fine-ass man of yours before I try to bring him over to the dark side." He winks, moving to the side and waving me out the door.

"I like you, Dall. Might just have to keep you around."

"I think I'd let you."

"Like you'd have a choice," I call over my shoulder.

Before I make it to the end of the short hallway, I'm attacked by Maura swooping me up in a strong hug.

"Don't hate me. Be safe. Have fun. Keep an open mind. I love you."

And just as fast as I was crushed in her embrace, I'm set free, being pushed into the living room. Hudson turns from staring out the patio door, smirking at me in that sexy way of his.

"Hi." It's almost shy, the way he says it. It's…cute.

"Uh, hi."

He strides over to me, raising a hand to just one side of my face. I can't help it—my head rolls into his simple touch. My breath hitches as he inches his lips closer to mine, only to swerve at the last second, placing a gentle kiss on the corner of my mouth. Instead of pulling away, he shocks me by ghosting his lips across my cheek, his hot breath sending chills down my spine.

"You look beautiful."

I gaze up at him as he pulls back, smiling at the glint I see in his eye. *He noticed my outfit.* I love that he didn't outright say something about it, but instead subtly acknowledged its significance, just as I had done by wearing it.

Hudson glances down at my mouth, back to my eyes, and then straight back to my lips again. Taking the initiative, I stand up on my toes and press a small kiss to his lips.

"I don't normally kiss on the first date, but I'll make an exception for you," I tell him, winking as I move away and head toward the door.

I grab my jacket and purse off the back of the couch and turn back to him. "You coming, Casanova?"

"Goddamn I've missed that mouth."

"So, where are we headed?"

We're buckled in the car, racing down the highway out of town; my interest is officially piqued.

"Somewhere."

"Right. I can see that. But where?"

"Can't you just enjoy the surprise?"

"Going off all your other awesome surprises lately, no."

He winces at my words, but I refuse to take them back, especially since they're true.

His sigh tells me I've won this round. "Well, if you *must* know, I've made some arrangements. We're, uh, going out of town for the weekend."

Out of town? To where? Wait…why?

"Um, right. Okay." I wring my hands together in nervousness, unsure of what he's planned. "Uh, where are we headed to?"

I'm watching him, so I see the hesitant sidelong glance he shoots my way. He licks his lips, drawing out the moment another few seconds. "The beach."

"*The* beach?"

He squints one eye closed, like hearing the words leave my mouth makes him question everything. "Um…yes?"

I sit back in my seat, not realizing I'd moved forward at all. "Oh."

"Does that worry you? Are you mad? Should I cancel the trip?"

Am I mad? No. Worried? A little. Cancel the trip? I *think* the answer is no on that one as well. The nerves creep in, making me want to say yes, but I know this could be a good opportunity for us. A chance. One to start over. And despite how going back to the beach where his daughter almost died on my watch nearly a year ago makes me want to vomit all over his pretty SUV, I think this will be a good thing for us.

At least I hope it will be.

"No, don't cancel. Let's go."

He lets out a relieved breath. "Good." He nods a few times. "Good," he repeats.

"Good."

"We have such a way with words."

"I do. Not sure about you though."

"See? Sweet talkin' me already. I knew this was going to be a good trip."

I roll my eyes. "Whatever. You *hoped* this would be a good trip. You're lucky I even said yes to this surprise adventure."

He quiets down and lowly says, "Thank you."

I bravely reach over and grab his hand, turning it over and lacing mine with his. "We've got some work to do this weekend, Hudson. With ourselves, with us. I…I don't want to give this up. And I realize now I was wrong to walk out as suddenly as I did. I should have stayed and listened to your reasons, not because I owed it to you, but because that's what you do in a relationship. I fear I've let my fucked up head twist shit around, and that's not okay."

I pause, taking a moment to let that sink in, not only for him but for me too. That's the first time I've admitted that out loud. It's scary, but it's truthful. I *have* twisted things in my mind. I've begun to question absolutely everything about our relationship, and that's not fair to either of us.

"We need to heal. I think this little getaway of yours might help."

He squeezes my hand a few times. "I sure as hell hope so."

The ride is shorter than I remember from last time, and before I know it, we're pulling up to the faded yellow beach house, complete with white shutters and a rackety wooden, unpainted fence. It needs a little TLC, sure, but it's perfect.

"This place is just as beautiful as I remember."

Hudson climbs the stairs behind me lugging our bags with him. Maura managed to sneak mine to him when Dallas was calming me down in the bathroom. Their scheme is a little irritating, but I don't have it in me to be mad over something I desperately needed. In fact, I'm rather grateful for it. She may have pushed us but at least she pushed in the right direction—together.

We clamor through the front door and take a moment to let the house air out before we close it again. Hudson heads down the hallway toward the bedrooms.

"Wait. Joe's not here. Does this mean *we* actually get the big bedroom this time?"

I take note of his use of "we." It makes me…nervous. We haven't slept in the same bed since the night before I walked out. While I've missed that, I'm also a little scared to take that big step. But if we're playing house this weekend and attempting to mend the cracks in our relationship, we need to go big or go home.

"Huh. I suppose *we* do."

He smiles at my words, and it's one of those heart-stopping smiles. I can't help returning it.

Hudson walks our luggage to the big bedroom and I find myself standing in front of the large French doors, mesmerized by the wavy beach that's our backyard. The last time we were here changed our lives dramatically. I can only hope for the same this time around. If not, I feel like this could possibly be our last shot at…well, us. I don't want that. I want forever with Hudson.

And I know how unrealistic and cheesy that sounds, but I've always believed that if you want something hard enough and work at it with all you've got, you can make it happen. That's what I'm determined to do here.

Strong arms snake around my waist, holding me captive in a warm embrace. I lean back into Hudson, letting him hold us both up.

"I'd suggest us trying to do something romantic like cooking dinner together, but with our track records in the kitchen, I don't think that's such a good idea. I kind of like this beach house and prefer to not see it as a pile of ashes."

I twist a little, peeking over my shoulder at him. "I can see your faith in my cooking abilities hasn't waned."

He smirks. "Never."

God, I've missed that smirk.

"So, dinner out?" I ask, turning back around.

"Naturally." I feel him bend down, his lips grazing against my neck as he speaks. "Or we can order in."

"Was that code for *Supernatural* and chill?"

He groans playfully and buries his head in my neck, his laughter vibrating against my body. "I love how you know me."

I laugh and turn around, wrapping my arms around his neck. "You just love me in general."

He looks a little surprised by my words, and I have to say, so am I. We fell back into our normal banter and routine in just a matter of moments. It's almost as if the past year of his lies haven't even happened, like we haven't spent all these days apart. It feels like nothing and everything has changed. All at once. In the best way possible. I feel…lighter. I feel…forgiving. I feel ready to move on.

"This is true," he whispers before pressing his lips against my forehead, my favorite move of his. He holds his lips there for a few seconds before he slowly begins to trail feather-light kisses down my nose and straight to my lips. He doesn't press, he just holds his lips to mine. It's simple and perfect.

All it takes is the unconscious act of wetting my lips, my tongue brushing against him, and he attacks. He presses his lips to mine—hard. Our mouths meld together and I open for him when I feel his tongue trace the seam of my lips. They wage war against one another. Only it's not bloody and violent. It's full of beauty and heart. It's a war of love, and we're both waving the white flag right now.

He pulls back some and I lazily open my eyes to meet his swirling green-blue gaze. The look he's giving me is full of questions, but I know the most important one. And the answer is yes.

Yes, I want this.

Yes, I'm ready to fight *for* him rather than against.

Yes, I want to move on.

Yes, I forgive him.

Yes, yes, yes.

Something's changed over the last few days. Us talking again, the last encounter we had in his office, the drive over here, the talk I had with Elle. It's as if the moment he said we were coming here, I gave in. This place, what it represents to us, to *me*…it means something. It means new beginnings. And I think that's what he had in mind the entire time. Just by being here, breathing in the salty air, surrounded by the time we saved each other and didn't know it, things are different. Things are better. And I'm ready to do what my heart's been screaming at me from the beginning.

This is it. Hudson is *it*.

I don't need to say anything; he knows. His lips fall back to mine and his hands find my face, sweeping up into my hair, grabbing hard onto my head and pulling me into him. I grab at him, bunching his shirt into my fists. He stumbles a little when I push him backward until he reaches the couch. He falls into the sofa and I crawl onto his lap. He pulls me back to him, capturing my lips with his once again. He gently tugs at my shirt and I lift my arms, leaving me shirtless and straddling him. I can feel his dick straining against his jeans and I push down some; he pushes back. We stay like that for several minutes, grinding against one another, kissing until our lips are numb.

Breaking the kiss to peel his shirt off, he holds on to me, flipping me to my back and settling himself between my legs. We adjust ourselves until he's back to rocking against my sweet spot and I let out a soft moan.

"I miss this," he says, kissing at my neck, lightly biting down in just the right spots. "I missed the way you feel, those sexy noises you make, the way your eyes light up whenever you're horny."

"I miss you not talking during our sexy time," I tell him, gasping when he once again hits that special spot.

He just chuckles against my neck and does it again. "Rae…"

"Hudson," I mock. "Shut up. Take your pants off already."

He doesn't argue, sitting up to unbutton his jeans, pushing them off his hips and shuffling the denim down his legs.

"Really? You couldn't just get off the couch to do that?"

"And miss annoying you? Never."

I can't even pretend to be annoyed by him. I've missed this too much. The way we work together applies to every aspect of our relationship. We can laugh and joke during sexy time and still completely *feel* it. So far it's no different after our time apart.

He unbuttons my pants, pausing to arch an eyebrow at me. "Am I allowed to undress you *on* the couch? Or did you want us *both* to stand up for this?"

"Just take my damn clothes off, Hudson!"

Laughing, he complies. He peels my jeans down my legs, taking his time, enjoying me squirming beneath him just a little too much. Once we're both down to just our underwear, Hudson pauses, his eyebrows scrunched together.

"Problem?" I question, unsure what's made him suddenly stop.

"I…I don't want to fuck you on the couch. It seems…wrong after everything."

"Then take me to the bedroom and fuck me."

He shakes his head. "I… No."

I groan, throwing my head back into the couch cushion. "You're such a tease!"

"This conversation seems strange. Shouldn't, by most people's standards, I be the one that's begging for sex?"

"Fuck most people. They're wrong. Women love sex just as much as men. Especially if it's good sex. Which is what it is with you. So, let's get this show on the road. I'm *dying* over here, Hudson."

He leans down and places a tender kiss on my lips and then doesn't move away. "I'm not fucking you, Rae. I'll gladly bring you to whatever release it is you need right now, but I refuse to just fuck you. I want to make love to you. Sweet, slow love. Later. I want to do this right."

His words melt through my frustration and my heart picks up its pace. Hudson's words reach into my heart, my soul, and settle there, weighted down by the love shining so bright in his eyes. I get it. I get *him.*

I reach up and kiss him, slowly, seductively. "I love you."

He stills at my words. Then he's moving, pushing against me, bringing his hands up to cradle my head, caging me in his arms. His full weight falls onto me and I've never felt so complete. The feel of his lips against mine is raw and real, harsh yet gentle. It's perfect.

That's how we stay, tangled together on the small space kissing, talking, stroking. It's hours of contentment, of bliss, of love.

Chapter Thirteen

HUDSON

After our multiple make-out sessions and hours of relaxation, we decide it's time to actually move off our asses and get food.

"Do you want to try the Mexican place or just burgers from that 'World Famous' place?"

"Burgers are fine," Rae calls through the bathroom door adjacent to the bedroom.

I'm sitting on my bed, scrolling through my phone looking for different restaurants while she dresses and does whatever other girly shit she's doing to get ready for dinner. It all feels…normal. And I've fucking missed normal.

She comes strutting out of the bathroom in a dark pair of jeans hugging her curves and a black top that slinks off one shoulder. She looks stunning as always. Glancing up at me with those dark green eyes of hers, I can see that she's looking at this in the same way I am—a step forward. We're both looking to move on. Not that we don't have a lot to talk about and shit we still need to work out, but we're agreeing to work on it. Together. That's the most important thing right now.

"Goddamn. You're beautiful." Her cheeks turn a bright red, something they hardly ever do. Standing, I walk closer to her, bending slightly to place a small kiss on one of her inflamed cheeks. This makes her blush even harder.

Rae peeks up at me, her eyes sparkling. "Thank you."

I give her a smirk. "No, thank *you.*"

She laughs. I fall in love just a little bit more.

"You ready?"

"I'm always ready for you," I tease, waggling my eyebrows up and down.

"You are quite full of yourself today, huh?"

"There are other things I'd like to fill."

"Hudson Michael Tamell! You did not just say that!"

"Oh, but I did." I bend down closer to her, my lips brushing her ear. "And I meant it."

Straightening back up, I move around her and out of the bedroom, smiling to myself at the sputtering I hear from behind me. She can act all offended or surprised if she wants, but I know she's enjoying this as much as I am.

We make our way to the car and travel the short journey to the only reputable burger joint in town. We seat ourselves and settle down to glance over the menus.

"I'm ordering two of everything and making you pay. Just for that little stunt you pulled earlier," she says from behind her menu.

I look up and meet her eyes when she glances at me from over the top. She doesn't have to lower the menu for me to know she's smiling. I can see it in her gaze. I've missed that look.

"That's fine. You just order whatever your little heart desires. My treat."

She huffs at my lack of response. I'm not letting her win this game. I'm enjoying having the upper hand too much to let that happen.

The waitress comes to the table to take our drink order. She starts with Rae.

"I'll take a large chocolate shake." She looks over at me with a devious grin. "He'll have one too."

I groan. She knows I can't handle chocolate in large amounts like that. But I let her get away with it and pretend nothing is amiss. Then she proceeds to order me a veggie burger with broccoli as my side while she gets the Bacon Bacon Bacon Burger *and* extra French fries. With cheese. Again, I say nothing. Because by not reacting, I'm winning. And she hates it when I win.

So, I dutifully eat my veggie burger—which is quite tasty—and pick at my broccoli with tested patience and love. She's so close to winning with that move.

We make small talk and stare daggers at one another during the entire meal. Then, when I'm only about halfway through my meal, she declares she's done and demands we leave instantly. I don't argue with her. We pay and leave. I steer the car the opposite way, taking her to a small cove just up the road.

"Where are we going?"

"Didn't we have this same conversation when I picked you up from Maura's?"

"No," she responds, matter of fact.

I roll my eyes at her stubbornness. "Okay, then wasn't it something extremely similar?"

"Yes."

"And do you remember how that conversation went?" I glance toward her and she nods. "Then just repeat that. Ya know, minus you throwing stones at me about lying. Let's leave that part out, huh?"

Sighing, she relents. "Fine. Surprise away, mister master of surprises."

After another mile or two, I pull off onto the side of the road and instruct her to follow me. I stop at the back of the car, grabbing a blanket and small cooler, and head down the shallow embankment with her on my heels.

"Hudson, where are we? What are we doing here?"

I ignore her questions and keep moving forward, knowing she'll follow. Once I find the perfect spot, I spread out the blanket and set the cooler down, pulling Rae down along with me until we're cozied up together with her between my legs.

"What is this?" she asks sweetly.

I take a moment to respond, enjoying the view before me and the feel of her in my arms. I take in the ocean and its beauty, the sunset reflecting off the waves, casting an orange hue to everything around us. This moment is serene, and everything I'd hoped for.

"This is us, Rae. This is our time. Our re-do. Our new beginning. This is how it should have happened the first time."

"How what should have happened?"

I don't respond because the moment isn't right yet.

She sighs, knowing I'm not going to give anything up. Rae leans back into me, making herself comfortable in my embrace. I squeeze her tighter, afraid that she and this moment are going to disappear any second.

"How's Joe?"

"She's good. I swear she gets taller and smarter every day. She's with my mom this weekend. Surprisingly, she didn't even ask to come along. Something about a girls' day Nanna promised her."

"I miss her."

"She misses you too."

"I miss you."

My heart swells at her words.

"I miss you more."

We sit, quietly, and watch the sun set over the glittering water. We don't leave when the clouds cover the sky and leave only the light of the moon to illuminate the area around us. Not even an inch is taken when the bugs start biting at our skin and we start to shiver from the cold. No. We just…sit. And enjoy the moment.

"Rae…"

"Hudson…"

"Are you… Are we…" I can't seem to get a full sentence out and my throat is suddenly scratchy. I sit up some, shuffling her back a little, searching around for the cooler. Rae sits forward, giving me room to grab a bottle of water. I chug at least half of it until all the stickiness is out of my mouth. The words should be able to easily glide past my lips, but…they hesitate. Again.

"Hudson?" she presses.

Licking my lips, I try again. "Where are we, Rae?"

"The beach?"

I smirk at her. "I only missed your mouth sometimes."

She laughs, but it's a short one. It's almost like she's too afraid to enjoy the moment now. Scared of what's about to happen. I am too.

She lets out a sharp breath. "I…don't know, Hudson. I wish I had all the answers here, but I don't. I know I want to move on. I want to move forward. I want to… Fuck. I just want you, okay? Can't that be enough for now?"

Closing my eyes against her words, I bite my tongue. Physically, not metaphorically. Honesty, right? That's what Rae's after. So I give it to her.

"No."

"Huh?"

"No, that's not enough, Rae." She turns toward me, giving me her full attention, her face scrunched up in confusion. I meet her stare.

"Look, I fucked up. I've admitted that. Several times. I've also apologized several times. I need to know what the future holds for us. Not that I'm giving up, because I swear to you, I won't. But I need to know."

Radio silence.

"I did it for you. For you, Rae. I know I shouldn't have lied. I get that loud and clear. I just can't apologize for wanting you to have a relationship with your father that I never got. All I can ask is that you try to see it from my perspective. You don't even have to understand it all at once. I just want a chance, an inch at a time even, because I'm dying over here."

She takes a deep breath before she answers me, almost like she's choosing her words *very* carefully. I don't know how I feel about that. I do know that my heart leaps at the single tear that runs down her cheek, at the look of pain that etches itself into her features. I want to wipe away the tear, wipe away our past, our hurt. But I can't.

"You don't think I died a little when I found out about your lies? Your *repeated* lies. You think it doesn't still hurt?"

"I know it does, Rae. I know it. But you have to let me help you heal."

"How?"

"Let me love you again."

"I haven't stopped, Hudson. Not a day has gone by where I haven't pined for you, where I haven't cried myself to sleep at night at how cold I felt without you there. Not one day has been spent without wanting you or loving you. And that's not going to change. I swear to you, I won't stop."

I wipe at my face, at the tears I don't realize I'm shedding. "I wish I didn't do that to you. I wish I could take it all back, that it never happened. But it did. And we have to work through that. Are you ready to? To move on?"

"Yes." Her answer is swift and sure. Exactly what I wanted to hear.

"Then what's the problem?"

"I don't know, dammit! I don't know!"

"Marry me," I blurt. "Marry me. Work with me on this. Work *through* this with *me.* Spend your life with me."

"I plan to, Hudson. I do. Just not yet. I'll gladly come home, but I'm not ready for *that* just yet. I still need some time for something that heavy."

I stare down at my lap, taking in what she just said. I get it. I understand where she's coming from on that front. And deep down, I know she's right. Getting engaged right now would be an act of desperation. That's not how I'd want to start this. That perfect moment Ted told me about weeks ago? This isn't it. I should have known.

"Is that not enough?" she whispers, mistaking my silence for something it's not. "Is that not what you wanted to hear?"

I look up at her. "No, that's perfect. That's *right.* I was wrong. Again. I'm just mentally berating myself for proposing out of line. Again. I suck at this."

She laughs lightly, scrubbing her hands down her cheeks. "Yeah, you kind of do. Come here." Rae leans up on her knees, stretching over to me and pressing a kiss to my lips. "I love you, Hudson. And I want that. I want forever with you. I really mean that. I just want that moment to be perfect. So far, it's not been. But we'll find that again. We'll find those little moments we had, and one day, we'll be us again. We just need to work toward it."

I gather her in my arms and lie back, pulling her until she's on top of me, stretched out. I wrap my arms around her as she lays her head on my chest right over my heart.

"I'm sorry," she says quietly. "I shouldn't have walked out on you when I did. I feel like I messed some shit up for us that shouldn't have been messed up with that move. I mean, this really is all your fault, but it was unfair of me to punish Joey like that too. You, on the other hand, totally deserved it."

I laugh because this is typical Rae. Straight to the point. This is the her I love more than anything in the world.

"I'm sorry, Rae. So fucking sorry. I hope one day you'll be able to understand it all from my point of view."

"I'm going to try."

We spend two hours lying on the blanket, watching the waves knock against one another like an aged whiskey knocking against the inside of a barrel—smooth and natural.

It's almost midnight when we enter the beach house for the second time today. A sense of peace had settled over us at the beach, but tension revs high once we're faced with choosing our sleeping arrangements. If it were up to me, I'd choose naked and tangled up in the sheets. I have no idea what Rae wants.

"So…"

"So…" she repeats.

"Are we, uh, heading to bed?" My cock aches at thoughts of us in the king-sized bed. I want so badly to wrap myself around her, to be inside her again.

She takes a step toward me. It's a steady, sure step. A step I take as a sign. I move toward her, trapping her, and she retreats, backing into the wall. I cage her in with my arms braced on the wall, dipping my head to run my tongue the length of her neck. She arches into my touch and grabs at my sides, pulling me into her. I settle my weight against her, giving into her silent begging. I pull away and strip my shirt off; she sighs. I fall back onto her, crushing my lips to hers. I beg for entrance with a trace of my tongue; she grants it. I grind my lower half into hers; she grinds back. It's a game of push and pull between us, and right now we're both winning.

"Bedroom," she states, dragging her mouth from mine with reluctance.

We stumble our way down the hall, not wanting to let go of one another long enough to walk there carefully. By the time we make it, I know I'm going to wake up sore after banging both of my knees on two different tables and stubbing my toe on the doorjamb. But none of it matters, none of it registers. The only thing I can feel right now is Rae and her warm body pressed against mine.

Rae bumps into the bed and abruptly sits, her hands going to my zipper immediately. She pops open the button and we work together to drag them down my legs. I stand before her, my dick proud and ready to go. She stares up at me and her look is lustful…heated…filled with love.

"Why am I the only one without clothes?"

She lifts a shoulder, a coy smile playing at her lips. "You've got your boxer briefs on. Not that they leave much to the imagination, but still."

I squint my eyes into slits. "Doesn't count."

She lets out a playful sigh and begins pulling her top off. "So technical," I hear her mutter. She pushes back on the bed a little more and shimmies off her jeans, leaving us even in the clothes department. Or lack thereof.

Rae lounges on her elbows in an unintentionally sexy pose, looking up at me with that sexy smile still in place, her breasts on the verge of falling from her bra, and her hair in disarray. "Happy now?"

I crawl up the bed, fitting myself between her legs until she drops down on her back. She winds her arms around my neck, but I don't want that. I grab them and hold them firmly to the bed above her head. Giving her a small kiss, I say, "Stay."

I run my lips down her chin, over her neck, and straight down until I reach her heaving chest. Her breasts brush my face with every harsh breath she takes. I push the cup of her bra aside and run the tip of my tongue over her right nipple. She inhales sharply, arching off the bed to press into my touch.

Chuckling, I pull back some and whisper, "I thought those weren't 'hooked up'?"

"I'm so fucking keyed up right now that *every* part of me is hooked up. I swear, you could probably tickle the back of damn knee and I'd orgasm."

I trail my hand down between us, pausing to swipe at the heat between her legs but not long enough to give her any sort of release. She arches into me again, but I keep moving, tracing an invisible pattern across her thigh, curling my hand around her leg right above her knee. And then I do just what she said—tickle right behind her knee. And damn does she react. She convulses, and laughter begins pouring out of her in waves.

I sit up and put my hands out in an act of surrender. "I can see my work here is done."

She laughs and pulls at me, bringing me back down on top of her. "You're such a smartass."

"Yeah, but I'm *your* smartass."

"You are."

The only thing that runs through my mind is that she said I was hers. *I'm hers.*

"Say that again."

"What? That you're a smartass?"

"No, not that. That I'm yours. Because you sure as fuck are mine."

Sadness creeps into her stare. "Of course you're mine, Hudson. There was never a moment where I doubted my love for you. I questioned my trust, but never my love."

"And now?"

"Now…"

Her hesitation sends my heart into panic. Now what? Does she still not trust me? Does she still see lies and deceit every time she looks at me? Because I can't live with that. I can't live without her looking at me and seeing hope, a future.

"Now I'm working on it. *We're* working on it. I love you, Hudson. I've already told you that won't change. Not now, not ever."

I kiss her, because for right now, that's good enough for me. Our lips fuse together in a heated moment and our bodies search for one another, seeking warmth and love. If the house burned down around us right now, we'd know the fire started right on this very bed.

I snake my arms around her and strip off her bra, not pausing as I pull down her panties. We part long enough for me to shed my boxer briefs and cover myself with a condom. Not even thirty seconds later, I'm back between her thighs, feeling her legs wrap around me like a blanket. There's not an inch between us, but it takes no time for me to slide right into the warm center I'm seeking. We create a beautiful symphony with every thrust and pant, glued together by sweat and the greed for release.

"Rae…"

"I know. I'm almost there."

I lift some, reaching between us to massage her clit, knowing it'll send her over the edge that I'm clinging to like it's my last hope. She lifts from the bed, back arched high, hovering for only a moment before crying out in pleasure. I can feel her spasm around my dick, every squeeze dragging me closer and closer to the edge. With two more thrusts, I follow her release, surrendering myself to the pull.

I collapse in a heap on top of her, conscious of my weight on her small frame.

"Hand to God, I just had the best fucking orgasm of my life."

She slaps my back. "Hudson! You can't say 'God' and 'fucking' in the same sentence. Or 'orgasm.'"

"Says who?"

"Me!"

Laughing, I roll off her, pulling her with me. She rests her head on my chest, snuggling closer into me. I kiss the top of her head, letting my lips linger because the last thing I want is to let this blissful moment go.

"You ruin all my fun," I say, brushing my lips against her head.

"You love when I do."

"I love you."

"I know."

Every time she's said that these last few weeks, I've had these odd aches in my chest like someone's there with a chisel, carefully carving those two words into my chest cavity. Slowly.

But now? Now it feels good. It feels hopeful. It's enough.

"We're good together, huh?"

I know she's not just talking about the amazing sex we just had, but us in general. And she's right. We have issues, that much is clear. But I think our willingness to work through them makes us strong—stronger than our issues. Even though Rae walked out and I fucked up, no matter how many times I felt those little fissures in my heart grow, I always knew we'd find a way back to each other. Because we've always done that. Shit, we technically spent almost twenty years apart and still—somehow, someway—we found our way back. As unintentional as it may have been, it happened. And it's led us to this moment. Despite the mistakes we've both made, the problems we've had, I wouldn't change where we're at right now for anything.

"We are."

"I think it's because of what happened on the beach all those years ago. You rescuing me."

"Why do you think that?"

"You saved me, Hudson. You gave me life. Shit doesn't get more intimate and ingrained in your soul than that."

I chuckle at her eloquent way of putting it. But I don't disagree.

"That could be the case. Or I could just be so amazing that you can't resist me."

"Or that. But I doubt it."

Shuffling around until I can reach, I smack her ass. "You're a shit."

"But I'm *your* shit." I lift my brows at her choice of words and she laughs. "Doesn't work there, huh?"

"Not at all."

I wake with a full heart and an empty bed.

Only one of them is satisfying.

Reaching over, I feel that the sheets are cold, like they've been abandoned for hours. *Where in the hell did she go?*

I sit, swinging my legs off the side of the bed. Panic washes over me like a tidal wave. It's quick and harsh, pressing on my chest. *Where is she? Did she change her mind? Is she not ready to move on? Fuck!*

It's almost as quick as the tidal wave crashes that a quick smack of shut-the-fuck-up-and-stop-being-dumb hits me. I ignore my idiotic brain, because I know none of that's true. She didn't change her mind. She's ready to move on. *We're* ready to move on. After the way we made love last night, there's no denying that. It wasn't a moment of goodbye; it was a new beginning.

I laugh to myself. A new beginning? We've had one before. Almost a year ago now, actually. After the accident involving Rae and Joey and almost losing them both, we started over. We built something new from scratch. So maybe this isn't another beginning. Maybe it's just the next chapter. Or even a second act. Either way, it's new, it's fresh, and it's what is needed.

Pushing myself from the bed, I go in search of Rae. I have a hunch she's out on the beach, standing there staring out at the ocean with the wind whipping her auburn hair around in a crazy-beautiful way. My suspicions are confirmed when I reach the full-length windows in the living room facing the shores. It's easy to spot the outline of her small stature standing just at the water's edge. Even from here I can tell she's deep in thought and can just imagine she's sporting that little crinkle between her brows as they're drawn together tight in concentration. I can't help but wonder what it is that's got her so pensive.

I take my time pulling on a shirt and jeans and slipping into my shoes, hoping to give her some more time to work through whatever it is that's bouncing around inside her head. I'd normally let her just go about her business and give her space, but with everything that's happened between us lately, I can't help wanting to know where her head is right now.

Following her footprints down to the beach, I stop short when I get close to her and admire the view in front of me. She's gorgeous, effortlessly so. A burst of pride and happiness raps on my chest at the thought that she's mine forever.

She must sense me approaching because she speaks before I even announce my arrival.

"I was wondering when you'd wake up."

I take the last few steps toward her, wrapping my arms around her waist from behind. She leans into my embrace automatically, sighing in contentment.

"How long have you been out here?"

She shrugs. "An hour or so." A small laugh. "It's a shame I've let my past fears keep me from the water all my life. It's peaceful out here. I think I'm a little in love with it."

"It's always been one of my favorite places. This exact stretch of beach, I mean. It's quiet and never gets crowded, even during the tourist season. It's the perfect place for a bonfire, cookout, party, or just a day of doing nothing. I'd always hoped that one day I'd be able to just pack up and move here permanently."

"A year ago, I'd have said there was no way in hell I'd do that. But now I highly doubt I'd put up much of a fight."

I kiss the top of her head, thankful for how hard she's worked to overcome her fear of the water. "Let's do it, then. Plan a future here with me, Joey, you."

"You forgot Rocky. And our new puppy."

She twists around to smirk up at me, at the confused look on my face. "We have a new puppy?"

"We will after you buy me one for being a jackass," she answers.

I can't help the laugh that escapes. "You're lucky I love you."

Turning back around, she burrows into my embrace even further. "I know."

She's quiet again, and I can feel some apprehension creep into her body. I squeeze her tighter, rocking back and forth a little, almost in an effort to shake out what's weighing on her.

Finally, after many more minutes of silence, I get the courage to ask. "What's on your mind?"

"I want to see my dad." Her response is so quiet that it almost gets lost in the wind.

"Okay. We can do that."

Turning in my arms, she rests her head against my chest, fitting so perfectly that I can rest my chin on her head. I feel her head shake before she even speaks.

"No, Hudson. I need to do it alone."

I sigh. Rae visiting with her father has potential to go south in a matter of moments. She's angry, he's hurting. They're both in a very vulnerable spot. I don't want her to be alone if it doesn't end well. I'm scared she'll turn what happens with him back onto us and run again. I can't bear that.

But in the end, it's not my decision.

"Okay." Another deep breath. "Okay. When are you thinking of seeing him?"

She pulls back and peers up at me. I know she's a little surprised by my reaction, but I can also see the appreciation shining from her eyes. My answer was most definitely the right one for her.

"Today."

"Like *today* today?"

"Is there any other today?"

"No."

"Then yes. I want to see him today."

She steps away from my embrace, and I don't miss the way she plants her feet into the sand just a little more, locking her legs in place, readying herself to stay firm on this. She doesn't need to, though. I won't argue with her or try to talk her out of it. If she thinks this is what she needs, then this is what she needs. I won't stand in her way.

"I need to say everything I need to say while I have the courage to do so. Today is when I have it. So it has to be now."

I give her a firm nod. "I'll go get the car ready."

Chapter Fourteen

RAE

I'm being tormented. By a fucking door.

It only took us thirty minutes to shower, dress, pack, and load the car for our trip home. Our ride was filled to the brim with deafening silence. But it wasn't a cold silence. It was as comforting as it was necessary.

I know Hudson is worried about my decision to go see my father, but my intentions are nothing but pure. I'm not going out of anger or hurt. I'm going for answers, for resolutions, for truths. We need to move forward, to bridge that gap we've created in our relationship. I'm finally ready to break out the tools to begin building. Maybe one day I'll even walk over it.

So here I am, standing on my father's doorstep, attempting to build. But I can't bring myself to start. I can't knock—my hands won't let me. I can't curl my fist or raise my arm or rap my knuckles. None of it is possible. I'm stuck.

And the door is fucking mocking me.

Before I realize what I'm doing, and purely out of frustration, I rear my leg back and kick the door hard enough to rattle. I cry out as pain races up my foot. *Fuck you, door!*

"Fuck!"

The inanimate object that's been teasing me for the past ten minutes opens up in a matter of seconds.

My father stands on the other side.

I can't help the surge of anger that passes through me. I want to scream and accuse and point every single finger I have at him. But I don't.

Instead, I clear my throat and speak to my father for the first time in almost a year. "Hi."

Hi? Yep, that's all I've got.

A smile ghosts his lips. "Hello."

Then we stand there. Staring. It's awkward, it's irritating, it's agonizing, and it's relieving. It's all these different emotions at once. It's overwhelming to the point of tears. But I refuse to cry.

He scratches at the short beard covering his face then opens the door a little more with hesitation. "Do you want to come in?"

I want to laugh at this entire situation. Last year, I'd have just knocked once and waltzed right into his house. I wouldn't have had to stand at his doorway with trepidation covering every action. However, things have changed. Majorly. This is just another side-effect of that change.

"Sure."

I move past him, not pausing in the entryway, and head straight for the living room. I pause when I see that he's gotten new furniture. Another change.

"Do you want something to drink?" he asks cautiously.

"No, I'm fine. I just… Can we get this over with?"

His shoulders sink at my words. I cringe because that came out sounding entirely too bitchy, and that's not how I meant it.

"Sorry," I start. "That didn't sound like it should have. I have things to say and the courage to do so right this moment, and I just need to get it out. That's all."

He nods. "I understand. I have things of my own to say. Want to sit?"

"Nice couch," I comment, taking a seat on it. It's comfortable. Actually, it's probably the only comfortable thing in this room. Everything else is suffocating, stiff, and unnerving.

I run my hands back and forth over the fabric, watching as it turns from a dark chocolate brown to a light mocha color with each stroke. It parallels life in a way. Like how just one simple act can impact things, changing them for everyone. I wish I could just wave my hand over it and change it back to a year ago, back to when things were simple, when I wasn't hurting so much.

"Rae?" My father's voice drags me from my thoughts. I turn toward him. "You wanted to talk?"

Folding my hands in my lap, I clear my throat. "I do."

I fidget, my confidence waning by the minute. I had it all planned out: storm the front door, demand to talk, say what I had to say, and leave. That was it. Nothing fancy, nothing dramatic. Sitting here now feels the exact opposite. It feels complicated, climactic.

"So…"

I jump a little, startled by his voice. It seems loud, though I know it's not.

"I want to start off by saying this: I love you."

Glancing up, I watch his eyes fill with tears that threaten to spill over.

"I…"

I hold my hand up, stopping him. "Wait. Please. Let me get this out."

He nods. I blow out a breath.

"I have had a lot of time to think about everything that happened last year. Sometimes, when I think about it, I get pissed. Sometimes I don't, and I understand why you kept my 'nightmare' as just that, as a dream. I've come to terms with what happened back then, when Mom watched me drown. I know she was sick, Haley told me."

He doesn't react to that confession. I assume Hudson told him my sister and I have been on speaking terms for the past nine months or so.

"I never truly blamed her for taking her own life, but I have always wondered what led to it. It all makes sense now. There was a brief moment where I felt responsible, that what transpired on the beach is what led her over the edge, but I don't think that anymore. I'm a little grateful for that part of everything, for believing it was a dream all these years. Because I *would* have felt that growing up. I'd have believed it was my fault she was gone. I'm old enough now to know the difference. I feel like I've been spared that particular kind of pain."

I pause for a moment, dabbing at my eyes with the backs of my hands, trying to keep the tears at bay. I can see that my father is openly crying now. It hurts. But so does what's happened.

"So I guess I'm saying thanks," I continue. "Thanks for sparing me, for trying to help me. I don't fully agree with it, but I understand it. I get it. You didn't want me to feel at fault. Thank you."

He acknowledges me by nodding, but not speaking yet.

"Now on to the anger. I'm mad. So damn irritated, Dad. It's like every horrid dream I had for all those years is swimming around inside of me. I hate it, and it's so hard to not want to direct that anger at you because you're here. But again, that day isn't your fault, just how you handled it is. I wish I had a better way of explaining that. I know it sounds like a mess, and that's because it's still all jumbled up inside here." I hold my finger up to my temple. "I'm still working through it all."

Lowering my hand, I go back to petting the couch, amazed again at how it relates to our conversation. *I'm* the one controlling the changes, how the couch changes with my touch. That choice was taken from me all those years ago. I didn't get to deal with my problems myself. I didn't get to choose how I handled my mother's suicide or my drowning. I was young, so decisions were made for me. I can't help but wonder how different I'd be now if I'd have felt more loved by her, if I'd have understood why she pushed me away so much. I'll never get the chance to change how angry and neglected I felt, and it's saddening that I carried those feelings for so many years. She didn't deserve it. If I knew back then what I know now, I doubt I'd be feeling this now.

I'm quiet long enough for him to speak.

"I'm sorry if I ever made you feel like your mother didn't love you, that I didn't explain better what was ailing her. I should have. You should have learned of Erin's problems from me, not Haley. That was unfair."

I whip my head toward him at his words. *Unfair? What's unfair is being lied to!*

"Why did you lie to me? For all those years, why lie? Why not ease me into the truth? Why keep up a façade? Especially when you knew how much those dreams haunted me?"

"I was trying to protect you, Rae."

I spring from the couch, pacing the length of the couch in frustration.

"Protect me? I don't need protecting. I need honesty."

"You don't understand a father's need to protect his little girl."

"That's the same thing Hudson said."

"He's right. It's…it's indescribable. You have this urge to just twist her up in bubble wrap and never let her leave a white padded room. You want so badly to watch her grow into a smart, stable woman, but you also constantly look at her and see this fragile little girl, the one that begged to play dolls or paint your fingernails when she was six."

I smile at his reference to my old favorite pastime. I used to love painting my dad's nails. I wanted to make him as pretty as me, and that's the only way that made sense to me back then. I worshipped my father. He was my role model, my savior, my champion.

If I'm being honest with myself, I can see what he means. Joey may not be my daughter, but I feel that way too. I want her to look at me and see someone she can aspire to, someone she can go to for anything, someone who's going to save the day for her. So, I understand on some level.

No matter what though, it doesn't excuse lying for so damn long. Nothing does. It wasn't fair to me or to Haley. It wasn't right.

But it's also not unforgivable.

"How can I fix this, Rae? How can we get back to where we were before?"

"Before you lied to me my entire life?" He flinches at my venomous words. "We can't, Dad. That's not possible."

The sadness that weighs on him is evident as I watch his shoulders deflate for the second time since I've arrived.

"We can't go back to where we were before. But we can begin moving forward, we can rebuild. Not every bridge that's destroyed is replaced with an exact replica, and that's okay. Most of the time something stronger comes from the rubble."

He smiles. I smile. And something clicks. I feel it in that exact moment; we begin to heal.

"How'd it go?"

I close the door behind me and move around Hudson's intruding frame blocking the front door, making my way to the living room. I throw myself onto the couch, completely drained from all the highs and lows I've felt in the last few days. It's been an emotional roller coaster since I woke up for my date with Hudson. I'm exhausted.

"It was…okay."

"Okay? Just okay?"

"Yeah. It was okay."

He pulls at his hair, his nerves showing so predominantly I can see them hanging off his sleeves. "I don't know what that means. I don't know how to react to that."

I laugh lowly. "For starters, you can relax." He drops his hands with a grim grin. "I think we're going to be okay. It won't happen overnight. It's gonna take a lot of time and talking and effort from both parties, but I think we can work through it."

He expels a pent-up breath and sits down next to me. "You have no idea how good it feels to hear you say that."

"And you have no idea how good it feels to say."

"So you aren't still mad at him for secretly hanging out with me?"

This time I laugh loudly. "Oh, my poor confused man. I was never mad at him for that. Just you."

"Just me?"

I lift a shoulder nonchalantly. "Yeah. I mean, he'd already fucked up and lost my trust. You hadn't. You had all of it, actually. Then you tossed that shit right out the window."

"But you've forgiven me, yes?"

Narrowing my eyes at him, I say, "I don't know…"

He pretends to pout. "But I'm cute."

"Not good enough."

"I also got you something."

My eyes light up at the thought of a present. "A surprise?"

"Yeah, but I know you hate them. So maybe I'll just take it back."

Feet pound down the stairs and I swivel toward the noise.

"You cannot take me back! There's no such thing as a Daughter Store. Nanna told me so!"

I smile instantly at Joey's voice. She's home. *I'm* home. Then what she said sinks in.

"Wait. You told her that?" I quietly accuse Hudson.

He shrugs. "What? She was driving me crazy. I told her I'd take her back to the Daughter Store if she didn't stay quiet for at least five minutes."

"How'd that one go over?"

"It didn't. She started crying. Loudly, dramatically." He shudders at the memory. "It was terrible."

"You seem very scarred by this."

"Did I mention it happened in Target? Like, in public. In front of people. At the check-out."

I laugh, and it's like everything that's been dragging me down lately goes away for the time being. It feels good, natural.

Joey rushes through the room and jumps onto the couch, burrowing herself into me, hugging me tightly. I wrap my arms around her just as fiercely. Hudson wraps his arms around us both, pulling us into his strong embrace.

For the first time in a long time, I feel free, I feel happy.

I feel like I'm home.

Chapter Fifteen

HUDSON

Eight Months Later

"I knew she'd cave and say yes."

I turn toward the voice to my right. "How could she not? I'm me."

"Wow. I leave again for a month and you start sounding like this asshole," a second voice says from my other side.

"Tell me again why I thought it would be a good idea to ask you two to be my groomsmen?"

"Because the best man position was already filled and you felt bad that no one loves Tucker so you invited him?" Gaige says.

"I think you forgot your name was Gaige again," Tucker retorts.

"You're both impossible."

"You love us."

"That's a lie."

We all laugh, reveling in our crazy bond we share. With everything we've all been through in our short lives, I feel we've come out on the other side. We're doing well, all in stable relationships, and are all finally on the right career path. It's been a rough ride, but worth it.

A heavy hand falls on my shoulder and I look toward its owner. "I'm proud of you, man."

"Yeah? Well I'm prouder."

"And you're a jackass."

Gaige shrugs off Tucker's words. "This is true."

"But for real," Tucker says, "you've come a long way in your life. I've watched you grow from a scrawny moron to a semi-good-looking savvy business man. You have an amazing kid, who for some reason adores you, and a girl that blows all but my Maura out of the water. You're doing awesome."

I lift a brow at how he so intricately weaved together insults and compliments. "Uh, thanks?"

He claps my shoulder again. "Yeah, no problem, bud."

Gaige snickers from my other side and I have the urge to punch him in the stomach for it. Instead I settle for a verbal lashing. "Still prouder, asshat?"

He grins. "Definitely."

"It's time," Tucker says.

"You ready?" Gaige asks.

Blowing out an encouraging breath, I turn to face my future, my new life. "I'm ready."

We make our way back into the house only to get stopped by Maura in the living room, armed and ready with one of our mini instant Polaroid cameras.

"Don't move. I want to take a picture of this. You three look so handsome together."

"But I'm the cutest one, right?" Tucker tries.

"You're okay. Now, get together. The lighting is just right behind you guys."

We throw our arms around one another, and just when she's about to snap the picture, Tuck reaches out and slaps Gaige in the stomach, and I bust out in laughter instantly. I already know the print is a keeper.

"Okay, you're free to go. Wait! Where's the best man?"

"I'm here!" Joey comes rushing out of the back bedroom wearing a tuxedo t-shirt and jean shorts. She's adorable looking. "Ready, Freddy!"

"Wow, Joe. You almost look as ridiculous as Uncle Tuck does."

She beams at Gaige. "Thanks, Uncle G."

Gaige holds his hand out to high-five her for unknowingly being an accessory to insulting Tucker. I smile, loving how proud she is about her outfit no matter who teases her.

Joey frowns at his hand. "This is a fist-bump family. Who let you in here?"

This time everyone explodes in fits of laughter, partly because of what Joey said and the other part due to the disbelief coating Gaige's face.

Still stunned, he says, "Are you sure you're not mine?"

Joey just shrugs and moves toward the front door. "Last one down there is the biggest loser in the world!"

"Too bad that title already belongs to Gaige," Tucker quietly comments, sniggering to himself.

All I hear is a loud thwack as I follow Joey out the front door, my two knucklehead groomsmen hot on my heels.

We reach the beach and makeshift altar, pass through the small crowd, and take our places—me, Joey, Tucker, Gaige, and Dallas, who's become a good friend. Everyone gets a good laugh at how mismatched we look standing up there. While we're all wearing the same thing—the tuxedo shirt and a pair of shorts—we make absolutely no sense. A mechanic, an eight-year-old girl, a musician, a model look-alike, and a former line-backer.

I see Jane, a friend of both Rae and Maura's who I've just met, start pacing herself down the aisle. Next up is Haley, Rae's sister. Her eyes dart our way and I know who she's seeking out; I can't help but smile. There's a pause where no one walks, an empty spot in the bridal party for Perry while he's still in treatment for two more weeks after his minor setback.

When Maura begins making her way to us, Tucker bends down to Joey. "Still can't believe I'm letting you escort my girl for me, Bug."

Joey responds by punching his leg and I smother a laugh.

Finally, the crowd rises from their chairs as the music begins to swell. I let Rae pick all the music, so I'm fairly surprised when it's more of a normal song. I was expecting something epic and different. But this just goes to show that my girl can surprise me at any moment.

My first reaction is not what most people would expect. I laugh. Hard.

Because my girl, my Rae, my future wife, is wearing a goddamn Transit t-shirt on her wedding day. I fall for her just a little harder in this moment. She gives me a secret smile and loops her arm through her father's. I have a feeling our lives are going to be filled with secret smiles and laughter like this. And I can't fucking wait.

When they finally reach us, Ted bends down to whisper something in his daughter's ear. She nods, catching my eye, a mischievous spark hidden in hers.

He kisses her cheek and shakes my hand. "She's all yours, son."

"Thank you, Ted. For everything."

He claps me on the shoulder, bringing me in for a quick hug, and then takes his seat. Rae takes her place in front of me. The joy I feel right now can't compare to anything else. I never have to pay another bill in my life? It's about time. I just won a million dollars a year for the next fifty years? Neat. Give me all the money in the world, take away all of my worries, tell me I'm going to live for a thousand years. None of it compares to this moment. It's the only one that's mattered since my daughter came into this world.

Rae is becoming my wife. I feel full, complete, blissful.

Our officiant, Gary, instructs everyone to sit.

"I'm not gonna lie to you all, I'm terrible at this. Why these two asked me to officiate, I have no idea. I'm not eloquent, and flowery poems aren't my thing." The crowd laughs. "But I'm giving it a shot."

He pauses, looking us both in the eyes before he continues.

"Love can be beautiful." His eyes scan the group gathered, pausing briefly on the one who got away, Tucker's mom. "Love can be painful. It can be full of tears or laughter. It's anyone's guess as to which one you'll get. One thing love is—true, absolute love—is consistently unwavering. No matter the tears, no matter the painful days, it's always there and it's always going to win."

I watch as Rae's eyes fill with tears. I know well enough they're not sad tears, but proud ones. She's thinking about all the days we thought we'd lose each other, all the days we fought for what we have now. And she's remembering us winning. Because Gary is right—unconditional love always wins.

"And with what I've witnessed from you two, that's what you have. So, without further ramblings from yours truly, let's get this show on the road."

Our vows are simple, heartfelt, and ours alone. We each took the time to carefully write them out and it's shown in our words.

"You ready to do this shit?" she asks.

Laughing, I say, "I am. I think we've just started our married life indebted to Joey, but yes. I'm beyond ready. I love you."

She smirks. "I know."

We exchange our rings to the sounds of laughter ringing through the crowd.

"Well, guess my work here is done. I'm proud to introduce to you all, Mr. and Mrs. Tamell! You may now kiss your bride."

I step in close to her, wrapping my hands around her face just like I know she loves, and tilting my head. When our lips touch, it's like fire meeting oxygen for the first time—explosive.

And it was so worth the wait.

"Gary, my man, thanks for officiating. We appreciate it."

Gary shakes my hand and pats my back. "It's no problem at all, kid. I'm honored you even asked me. I…" He looks off over my shoulder as something catches his eye. "I've gotta go to talk to someone. Thanks again, Hudson. Not that I think you'll need it, but good luck with everything. You've got yourself a beautiful family."

He shakes my hand once again and heads off in the direction of where he was looking. I watch as he walks toward Joanne, Tucker's mom. Her face lights up as he nears her, and I wonder what's going on there.

"Can I have everyone's attention, please?"

I scan the crowd for my wife, finding her off to the side laughing with Dallas and Maura. Every time she smiles, I smile. Feeling my stare, she glances over at me and excuses herself from her friends, making her way to me. When she walks, it's like she's floating on air. It's delicate, precise, and almost angelic. The way she carries herself has always been one of my favorite things about her. Today, I swear she's walking a little taller, and I can't help but want to puff my chest out at the thought.

When she reaches my side, she wraps an arm around my waist and stands on her tip-toes to kiss my cheek. We don't speak because we don't have to. We both feel this odd swell of pride in knowing we're officially off the market and tied to one another now.

"It's time for the first dance. Who's ready?" Everyone cheers. "Good. Hudson, Rae, get your butts to the dance floor—er, dance sand! That was weird." He says the last line quietly, but the mic still picks up on it and we all laugh.

I look down at Rae and she shrugs. We didn't want to do the traditional wedding routine. Pictures, ceremony, first dance, cake, bouquet, yada yada…all that crap. We wanted simple and laidback. But I suppose Tucker had different ideas.

"We don't have to," I tell her.

"I know, but I kind of want to."

"But I suck at dancing."

"You do?! Shit, glad I didn't marry you for your dancing skills."

I laugh and pull her out onto the designated "dance sand" area.

"Right. So, this is a little not-so-traditional, and that's okay because neither are Rae and Hudson." Tucker brought the band he uses on stage as backup for our special occasion. He gathers them together and talks lowly with them while Rae and I awkwardly wait for them to begin. They all nod and go back to their places.

The familiar intro riff to AC/DC's *Highway to Hell* blares through the speakers, and the band struggles to play through their laughter, fizzling out before they even get through the first two lines of lyrics.

All I can do is shake my head and laugh until tears spill down my face at his antics. Because really? Who else would play that shit on my wedding day? No one but Tuck.

The band high-fives Tuck and leaves the stage. Tucker takes his seat on a stool with his acoustic guitar in hand.

"Alright, alright," he says into the mic. "Now this one is for real.

And this too is a little untraditional. I heard this beauty a while back and immediately thought of you two. It's called *Here's to the Heartache.* I mean, it sounds tragic, right? But it's not. It's full of hope. And that's what you two give me. That's what you give to a lot of people. You two, man, you've been through some shit. But you've persevered. Now look at you. Married! With an amazing daughter and a great future ahead of you. So, yeah, here's to the heartache and everything you've endured. It's led you here, and I can't think of a better place to be."

With that, Tucker begins crooning the song. I know right away it's going to be something I love. I wrap Rae up in my arms and we begin our dance, swaying back and forth, letting the music guide not just our movements, but our hearts.

"He's right. This does sound tragic," Rae whispers.

"It does. But I hear that hope."

"Me too."

We sway, moving together to the words and the melody. We're married. It's done. All the troubled times and hardships thrown our way, we made it through, came out victorious on the other side. We won. And we'll continue to do so.

"I love you, wife."

"I love you, husband."

"Is this where I'm supposed to recreate our New Year's moment and whisper 'here's to tomorrow' to you?"

Lifting her head, she looks up at me smiling. "Nah. This is where you come up with something new."

"Yeah, I think you're right." I press my lips to hers, lingering there for just a moment. Pulling away, I bend until we're cheek to cheek, until my lips graze her ear, and whisper, "Here's to forever."

Epilogue

Four Years Later

"HUDSONNNNNNNN!"

A drawn out name-screech? Not a good sign.

I run up the stairs two at a time, mentally pumping myself up the entire time, preparing for whatever tongue-lashing—that I probably deserve—I'm about to get.

"Rae?" I call out when I reach the hallway at the top of the stairs.

"Bathroom. Now."

I follow her seething words, gulping because *fuck* this does not sound good. I slowly creep into the bedroom, taking my time inching my way to the adjoining bathroom. I pause briefly outside the door. *Whatever it is, just smile and say sorry. Give that smirk she always falls for. You can do this.*

I push the door open and face my doom.

"Explain," she demands immediately, darting her eyes to the sink that she's standing in front of on the other side of the room.

I look toward it and see a white stick lying on the counter, not sure what it is from this distance.

"Umm…"

"Don't 'umm' me. Explain this shit." She huffs and picks up the object, thrusting it out toward me.

Slinking farther into the room, I start getting an inkling of an idea of what's got her so upset because what she's holding takes me back about twelve years, when I was sixteen and scared out of my mind. I have none of those feelings now.

I finally get within touching distance and grab hold of the stick she's shoving in my face. Looking down at it, I see two pink lines. And my life changes right in front of my eyes.

I glance back up at her, seeing a huge grin gracing her face. We've been trying for over a year to make a baby and it's been an uphill battle. But now, we've climbed it.

"We finally did it," she whispers.

I throw the stick aside and rush her, folding her into my arms. "We did it. We fucking did it."

"Literally," she teases.

"Holy fuck. I'm gonna be a dad again."

"And I'm gonna be a mom. Again."

I can feel the tears start racing their way down my face. My heart's making its own game, trying to beat harder and faster than it ever has before.

I kiss her head, her cheek, her lips. "We're gonna be awesome parents again."

She chuckles through her own tears. "Well, I am. Not so sure about you."

"Hey, Joe's a great kid."

"Only because I was able to intercept her at a young age."

Laughing, I rest my head against hers. I can't stop smiling, or crying, for that matter. I'm ecstatic. Everything I've ever hoped for has come true. My life, no matter how stormy and turbulent things got, is exactly what I always pictured it would be. I have a career I enjoy, a kid—now two—to dote on, and a wife who makes coming home every night my favorite thing to do. Nothing could make it any better than it is in this moment.

"I love you," I whisper before kissing her briefly.

I pull away and stare into the eyes of the girl who changed my life more than once, an equal amount of love filtering back through her gaze.

"I know."

THE END

Acknowledgements

My husband, The Marine, I love you. I am amazed by you every single day. The sacrifices you make for your country astound me. And this distance? This means nothing. It's going to be a blip on our radar in a few years. We're going to wade through the separations with ease. I know we will. Thank you. For being my partner, my constant encouragement, and for everything you do for us and our future. I love you. Always and forever. (P.S. You're the sexiest Marine I've ever met. Notice I said met. :-p)

sMother, you're my best friend. But don't tell people. I love you.

B, I miss you. For reals.

Murphy, as always, you're awesome. I could never thank you enough for everything but...thank you!

Jamie Walker, I love you. Okay? Okay.

All the Dawn's in my life. Dawn B., Dawn R., Dawn C., and Dawn D. You're all amazing friends and your support means so much.

Beth Thomason, I'm seriously out of words this time. I can't. Topping myself seems impossible. You're amazing. The best beta reader in this entire world. I love the way you push me, encourage me, and just tell me when I'm straight shit. You keep me going sometimes. Thank you.

#Murderface, Laurie, NikkiWhoWishesGaigeWasHers, and Amélie you guys are awesome! Thank you for all your help, listening to my stupid ideas, and for not being afraid to tell me when I'm wrong.

I refuse to give Colleen Hoover any sort of acknowledgement.

My BS family, do I really have to say anything to you assholes? No? Good.

To my family, by blood or marriage, your support means everything.

I know I'm forgetting people and that's because I suck. But…thank you all! For real!

Reader, thank you for all your support. It means more than you could ever know. I've loved writing Rae and Hudson like you wouldn't believe. I've watched them grow so much behind the scenes and hope you've enjoyed their journey. You'll see them again. I still have two books planned out!

With love and unwavering gratitude,
Teagan

Other Titles by Teagan Hunter:

Here's to Tomorrow

Here's to Yesterday

Here's to Forever: A Novella

Here's to Now

We Are The Stars

Want to be part of a fun reader group, gain access to exclusive content and giveaways, and get to know me a little more?

Join Teagan's Tidbits on Facebook!

Want to stay on top of my new releases?

Sign up for New Release Alerts!

TEAGAN HUNTER is a freelance cover designer by day. By every other free moment, a writer. She's a Missouri raised gal, but currently resides in North Carolina with her US Marine husband where she spends her days begging him for a cat. She survives off coffee, pizza, and sarcasm. When she's not writing, you can find her binge-watching various TV shows, especially *Supernatural* and *One Tree Hill.* She likes cold weather, buys more paperbacks than she'll ever read, and never says no to brownies.

You can find Teagan on Facebook:

https://www.facebook.com/teaganhunterwrites

Instagram:

https://www.instagram.com/teaganhunterwrites

Twitter:

https://twitter.com/THunterWrites

Her website:

http://teaganhunterwrites.com

Or contact her via email:

teaganhunterwrites@gmail.com

CPSIA information can be obtained
at www.ICGtesting.com
Printed in the USA
BVHW030003210420
577984BV00021B/153